DREAMS
—— *of the* ——
HEART

DAVID CRAIN

Copyright © 2022 David Crain.

All rights reserved. No part of this book may be reproduced, stored, or transmitted by any means—whether auditory, graphic, mechanical, or electronic—without written permission of both publisher and author, except in the case of brief excerpts used in critical articles and reviews. Unauthorized reproduction of any part of this work is illegal and is punishable by law.

ISBN: 979-8-88640-280-3 (sc)
ISBN: 979-8-88640-281-0 (hc)
ISBN: 979-8-88640-282-7 (e)

Because of the dynamic nature of the Internet, any web addresses or links contained in this book may have changed since publication and may no longer be valid. The views expressed in this work are solely those of the author and do not necessarily reflect the views of the publisher, and the publisher hereby disclaims any responsibility for them.

One Galleria Blvd., Suite 1900, Metairie, LA 70001
1-888-421-2397

1

BRADY WAS NINETEEN AND Chance was seventeen. The two boys were as close as two brothers could be. Chance idealized his big brother and always followed in his footsteps no matter where they led him, good or bad. Life on an Arizona ranch had made the two boys tough and mature beyond their years. Hard work was as natural as walking and breathing for them. Tough times made tough men and they lived during some of the toughest times and harshest country in American history.

The boys lived on the ranch with their folks, Thelma and Lewis Walker. It was a poor ranch so the only hired hand was one old man that had lived and worked on the ranch before either boy was born. He had been there so long that he was really like family and not a hired hand. Fact was he hadn't had a pay day in so long that he wouldn't know what one was. He would be insulted if you offered him money anyway. As far as he was concerned he was just old Uncle Hank. The ranch and those on it were his life and family.

He rarely left the ranch, didn't see the need as long as someone would bring him a bottle of whiskey once in a while. He did like his, Who-Hit-John; especially on occasions when the boys would come out after supper was over and set on the porch steps to listen to him tell stories of the old days. Days of Indians, cattle rustlers, and he even had stories of Cortez, the Spanish Conquistador, and gold in the mountains.

These were the stories that got the boys in trouble on more than one occasion. It always seemed like after a night of stories about Cortez that the boys would find the need for a camping trip to the mountains. Of course they would take their gold panning equipment and work the streams in search of the gold that old Uncle Hank had talked about. If they weren't panning for gold they would be searching the foot hills for the hidden treasure that Brady was sure was just waiting for him and his little brother.

Sometimes old Uncle Hank would go with them on these little adventures. He said it was to keep an eye on them. But in reality, he really wanted a chance to get in a little quiet drinking without Thelma making a fuss about his, "Unchristian", habits of drinking and cussing. And old Hank could throw out some words that could burn all the hair off your eardrums.

He would sit by the fire enjoying his whiskey while the boys were off looking for their gold. He would always have some supper on the campfire for them when they came in at the end of their day out looking for Cortez's gold. It might not be more than a pot of beans and a jack rabbit. Uncle Hank even made a pretty good tortilla if he hadn't hit the whiskey too hard that day.

Him and the boys would sit around the fire and eat their supper and Uncle Hank would drink his whiskey and tell stories. Hell, when you're ninety-three that's a pretty full day.

It was a time in America where the Depression was making hard times even harder for the ranches and farms that were used to going to the bank to borrow money when times were hard. The bank was broke the town was broke and all but dried up and blown away like a lonely old tumbleweed. And a lot of the ranchers that had borrowed money for a new tractor, or a new pickup truck, or whatever new contraption that they thought they needed, were in danger of losing their ranches. Some ranchers had already called it quits and loaded their personal belongings in a wagon or old truck and left whatever was left to look for something better. Few ever found it.

The Walker spread was one of the oldest and just about the only ranch is this part of the state that hadn't borrowed against the deed to their land to get all the stuff that most of the other ranches had in order to change with the times. As it turned out the Walker ranch was now in better shape than most because their land was free and clear the way it had been for a hundred years.

It seems that, up till now, Lewis was right in his die hard refusal to buy any of those fancy newfangled contraptions to do things that he thought a man and a mule or a horse could do just fine. A pair of horses and a wagon would get them to town just fine when they did have to make a trip to town for supplies. And those trips only had to be made once or twice a month because the Walkers were pretty self-reliant.

It's not that they were unfriendly or didn't enjoy other peoples company its' just that they raised their own beef, had their own chickens and eggs, had their own cows for milking and even made their own butter. And, as most others those days, they had a garden for raising vegetables. Thelma even made the Walker men their shirts. Times like these people made do with what they had.

Yea, as it turned out, Lewis Walker's stubborn streak is what saved him and his family from being swallowed up by The Depression like hundreds if not thousands of ranches and farms all across America. It well may have also been what got him and his family and ranch so far behind times that it would prove to be the struggle of a lifetime trying to catch up with rest of the world that had slowly left them behind. But then again, Lewis Walker was a man that had simple dreams and thought that family was a man's wealth.

It was 1932 now and the depression had taken its' toll on America. The Walkers were better off than most of their neighbors these days but were feeling the hardships just like everyone else. The price of beef was so low that a man couldn't afford to buy feed to fatten up the stock for market. So Lewis would have Brady and Chance move the cattle from one range to another.

This had to be done at least once a week because Arizona has more cactus and scrub brush than green grass. So the fat grain fed herds looked more like a bunch of mangy cactus eating wild cows than ever. Uncle Hank thought them damned cows looked even older and more worn out than he did. And that's mighty damned old and worn out he would say.

It was during a weekly moving of the herd to another pasture that Brady and Chance had their first run in with girls. You know those pesky girls that talk too much and know everything. The boys hadn't been around girls much except in school and at church on Sundays. And that had been a few years. On this day though, that was all about to change.

Today the boys, along with Uncle Hank, were moving the herd to the north pasture that ran along Wilson's creek. The creek was the property line between their ranch and the Wilsons. On this one particular day as the boys were checking out the brush and creek bank to be sure that their cows stayed on their side of the creek. Not that the Wilsons were an unfriendly bunch it's just that they were raised to respect other people's property, and especially property lines.

The Wilsons had four girls, Rachel eighteen, Jeni seventeen and the five year old twins Kari and Kali. Rachel and Jeni were out riding the creek bank as well that day on their side of the creek when they saw the Walker boys coming. The boys hadn't seen the girls yet so they hid in the brush until they knew for sure who it was.

Rachel said, "By cracky, if that ain't Brady Walker and his little brother what's his name." Jeni said, "Oh, his name is Chance", then she giggled and said, "I'd like to take a chance with him if you know what I mean big sister." They were both giggling so hard they could barely keep quiet.

As the boys got closer Rachel said, "Let's have some fun with these boys." She got up and told Jeni to follow her on down the creek real quiet like. So they snuck on down the creek a ways until they came to a deep spot that had brush sticking out next to the bank.

It was a warm day so they took all their clothes and got in the water and hid under the brush that stuck out over the creek. As the boys got closer the girls made some splashes in the water to get their attention but stayed hid until they were only about twenty feet away.

Then all of a sudden both girls jumped out of the water right in front of Brady and Chance showing them everything that their Maker had given them.

The boys were, to say the least, at a loss for words. Their eyes were so big that they couldn't have blinked if their life depended on it. If they had been walking instead of riding they both would have stepped on their bottom lips.

The girls are meanwhile jumping up and down and laughing and splashing water on the boys. It was Brady who was first able to speak when he said, "Ain't you two of the Wilson girls who used to pester us on Sundays at the church on Sunday?" Rachel just laughed and said, "Yea we are, but we're all grown up now Brady Walker, can't you tell?" Then they both giggled and turned around real slow to show them just why girl's jeans fit just a little different than boys did. Once again, big eyes and open mouths for the boys.

As Brady was wiping the sweat off his face, and doing his best not to stare, said, "Ain't you girls got any upbringing? It ain't proper for girls to be acting like you two are doing, it just ain't proper." Rachel put a pouty look on her face and said, "What the matter Mister High and Mighty Brady Walker?" and then with an evil little grin said, "Don't you like what you see?" Brady said, "Well I didn't say I didn't like what I saw, I mean no, I mean yes, well I don't know what I mean. It just ain't proper, carrying on like you girls are doing."

Brady turned his horse around and headed back the way they had come. Chance hadn't moved, blinked an eye, said a word or taken his eyes off them two girls the whole time.

Brady called for his little brother to come on but you might as well been talking to a rock for all the good it did.

Brady turned his horse around and went back and took a hold of the reins to Chance's horse. Chance was just staring at Jeni, who had come over real close to his horse and was smiling up at him, with a dumber than a frog look and grin on his face. Brady turned both horses around and headed back the way they came.

That was the hardest them Wilson girls had ever laughed. They would laugh every time they thought about this day for the rest of their lives. And it was also a day that the Wilson boys would never forget as long as they lived. And those two boys would look at life with a whole new set of eyes so to speak.

The boys made it back to where Uncle Hank had a fire going. He was fixing tortillas, had a pot of beans on the fire and had a Prairie Chicken on a spit over the fire and a half empty bottle of whiskey by now. The boys got down off their horses and walked over by the fire but neither one spoke as they sat down. Finally Uncle Hank broke the silence and asked, "Well, gald darnit, you boys lost your tongues, did you boys find any cows, or anything interesting, over at Wilsons Creek?"

The boys smiled and looked at each other, then Brady said, "Well Uncle Hank, I reckon you could say we done seen a, whole eye full, over at Wilsons Creek." Then both boys started laughing till tears came down their face and their sides hurt. Uncle Hank said, "Have you boys done got too much sun on your hat holders or did you both get some bad water out of Wilsons Creek?" Then the boys looked at each other and Brady said, "No sir, there's nothing wrong with the water over at Wilsons Creek, in fact, I reckon it's about the purrtiest water I ever did see Uncle Hank." Then they both started laughing all over again.

Uncle Hank just shook his head and said, "I reckon you boys been in the loco weed that my mule got in last year and darned near tore down the barn. Either that or you both done fell off your horse and bumped your head. I think I need me a shot of Who-Hit-John because you boys are giving me a powerful thirst". When the boys finally got their selves under control Brady told him the whole story about Wilsons Creek and the Wilson girls.

After Brady finished his story Uncle Hank just shook his head and said, "You mean to tell me those girls, didn't have on nuttin but what their Maker gave them?" Brady said, "Yes Sir, and maybe a touch of creek water too." They all laughed till they couldn't stand then Uncle Hank said, "I reckon that this calls for drink boys and after the day you boys have had I reckon it's about high time you boys had a drink too". So the three of them, proceeded to drink whiskey, eat beans, tortillas and prairie chicken. After they finished up with supper they set down around the fire while Uncle Hank told stories of Cortez's gold and passed around the whiskey bottle.

Early the next morning Uncle Hank was up bright and early and getting things ready to head back to the ranch. The boys were still asleep next to the fire with their heads under the covers. Uncle Hank got his shotgun and fired off both barrels real close to the fire to let the boys know that it was time to get up. It was a mighty long ride back to the ranch that morning.

On the way home Uncle Hank told the boys that it might not be a good idea to tell their Ma about the Wilson girls, or the whiskey drinking for that matter. So they all agreed that it would be best to keep what happened on this trip between the three of them.

Usually they only checked on the herd once a week when they were moved to a new pasture. But darned if those boys didn't work like their lives depended on it to get the daily chores done early each day so they could go over to Wilson's Creek to check on the herd. Well at least that's what they told their folks. But old Uncle Hank he knew better. Whenever Thelma would ask, "What in tarnation, are those boys up to?" Hank would say that they had seen mountain lions tracks up by Wilson's Creek and the boys were just worried about the cows. Thelma knew there was more than cow herding going on here but she didn't prod the boys too much. After all boys will be boys and she knew she had good boys.

Old Hank told Lewis the truth about what went on at Wilson's Creek the first day they got back. After all, he and Lewis had been working that ranch together almost fifty years. They had never lied to one another and Uncle Hank wasn't about to start now.

When Hank was done telling him about the Wilson girls, Lewis said, "You know Hank, those Wilson girls have done something to our boys that can't ever be undone don't you?" Hank just laughed and said, "I reckon you hit the nail on the head there Lewis."

The boys never did see the girls up by the creek again that week. But it wasn't because the girls didn't come to the creek, they were just hiding. They wanted to see if the boys would come to look for them. And sure enough they did. The boys must have ridden by that spot in the creek, where the girls had been skinny dipping, at least five times, that week. The boys had been bitten by the bug for sure. They had a whole different outlook towards girls now.

2

THE NEXT SATURDAY WHILE the family was setting around on the porch after supper talking and relaxing after a hard week of work on the ranch Brady and Chance set down next to their mom on the porch one on each side of her. After a few minutes Brady said, "Ma, when was the last time we went to town on a Sunday to go to Church?" Chance said, "Yea ma, we done got way behind on our praying and thanking the Good Lord for what he gave us."

Thelma looked from one boy to the other then she looked at Lewis. He just shrugged his shoulder as if to say he had no idea as to what the boys were up to. Then she gave Uncle Hank one of those looks that said, I smell a rat here. Old Hank he gave her a big old toothless grin and said, "You know, now that you mention it, I surely could use some preaching and gospel music to ease my old sinful bones." Then he got up and waddled off in that little shuffle of his giggling all the way to the bunk house.

Lewis said, "Well Ma, it has been a spell since we went to church, I guess it might do us all some good." She said, "I'll get everybody's Sunday go to meeting clothes ready." As she started to get up, both boys gave her a big kiss on the cheek then ran off into the house. She almost cried because she couldn't remember the last time one of the boys gave her a kiss let alone both at the same time.

The next morning everybody was up early. Lewis and Hank got the wagon ready while Thelma fried up some chicken and made a batch of buttermilk biscuits for a picnic after Sunday Services. The boys were doing their best not to get their Sunday clothes dirty or scuff up their freshly polished boots. They even had some stuff in their hair and it was all slicked down.

Reverend Hatcher was mighty pleased and surprised to see the Walkers there. Lewis shook hands with the reverend and said, "Well, what's it been about a year since our last visit to your good church?" The Reverend said, "It's been more like three, Lewis Walker." Lewis just hung his head and went on in the church. Thelma and the boys came up next and greeted the Reverend. He hardly recognized the boys they had grown so much. Then old Hank came up and shook hands with Reverend Hatcher.

The Reverend kept a hold of Hanks hand after they had shook and leaned over to where nobody could hear and said, "I'll take that bottle of whiskey you got hiding in your coat you old outlaw." Hank looked up at the reverend with a shocked look on his face, then, he gave the reverend a sly ole smile and said, "It was just a little holy water." But he handed his bottle over and started off inside. As he passed the Reverend, the Reverend said, in a voice that no one but him could hear, "I'll help you drink this after the service is over." That made Hank smile and off he shuffled to catch up with the rest.

Thelma enjoyed the sermon, Uncle Hank; well he got in a nice little nap while the boys were whispering back and forth to the Wilson girls setting in front of them. Thelma and Mrs. Wilson both had to give their kids one of those motherly looks that said, be quiet and pay attention.

Lewis just sat there and reflected on the ride into town in the wagon. They passed or were passed by all kinds of them newfangled, automobiles. There were cars and trucks and some big ole trucks too. One of them big trucks was loaded down with hay. Lewis thought, Lordy mercy, it would take him at least ten trips to haul that much hay. There was even a great big contraption they called a bus. Heck that thing must have had twenty people riding inside it. It was one of them bus contraptions that was making so much noise that it scared the horses so bad they were about ready to head back to the ranch.

Lewis started to realize just how far behind times the Walker ranch really was. Then he felt Thelma's hand on his shoulder. He reached up and patted her hand but was still lost in thought. Then he felt her shake his shoulder a little harder. Then he looked up and realized that he was the only one still sitting. Everyone else was standing getting ready to sing the closing hymn to today's service. Even Uncle Hank was up from his nap. Embarrassed, Lewis stood up and held one side of the songbook with Thelma and helped sing Rock of Ages with everyone else.

Reverend Hatcher shook hands with everyone as they headed outside the church. As Brady and Chance came by, the Reverend said, "Well how did you boys enjoy my sermon today?" He knew that they didn't have any clue as to what the sermon was about since they had carried on with the

Wilson girls the whole time. Chance started to say, well it was a, a, it was a, then Brady said, "It was mighty inspiring reverend, mighty inspiring", then pushed his brother out the door. Then Hank came by and the Reverend said, "How did you enjoy the sermon Hank, I hope it didn't interfere with your sleep." Hank said, "I was just a praying Reverend," then gave the Reverend a big ole toothless grin and shuffled on outside.

Thelma and Lewis came out next and stopped to shake hands with the Reverend. Thelma said, "Mighty fine sermon Reverend Hatcher." The Reverend said, "It's been a mighty long spell since you and your family have been here and I hope to see you all again real soon." Thelma thought about her two boys and those Wilson girls and said, "You know, I think you will see a lot more of the Walkers, and the Wilsons, in the future", then she smiled and went outside.

Then Lewis came up and shook hands and all he said was, "Times are changing Reverend, I reckon it's time us Walkers did a little catching up."

The reverend looked out in front of the church at the Walkers old wagon, it was the only one there, everyone else, had trucks or cars. The Reverend said, "I reckon you have said a mouth full Lewis Walker." Then Lewis shook his head yes and went on outside to find Thelma and that fried chicken.

There was a pond out a ways from the church and a lot of families had brought blankets and picnic baskets to do a little socializing while everyone was in town. When Lewis found his family, Uncle Hank was already on his second piece of chicken and his third buttermilk biscuit. Uncle Hank surely loved them buttermilk biscuits.

Lewis went and stood next to his wife who was quietly watching her boys over talking to Rachel and Jeni. She said, "They ain't my little boys no more Pa, their grown men ain't they?" Lewis put his arm around her and said, "That's a fact Ma, times are changing and I think it's about time we did some catching up with the rest of the world." She looked up at her husband with teary eyes and said, "I think your right Pa, but I do believe that part of the world has done caught up with our boys", as she looked over at her boys and the Wilson girls. Then Lewis had some chicken and biscuits and went off to catch up with what was new with some of the other ranchers.

Brady and Chance had moved off from most of the crowd with Rachel and Jeni to stand under an old tree where they could talk in private. The boys mostly just stared at the ground, the tree, or just about anything but look the girls in the eyes. Or look at anything for that matter because that day at the creek was all either one of them could think about. After a few moments Rachel finally broke the silence. She said, in a hurt little girl voice, "Why Brady Walker you haven't said one word about my new dress. Don't you like it?" Brady looked up and said, "Well I guess it's about as pretty a dress I ever seen."

Then Chance, following his brothers' example, told Jeni that he thought her dress was pretty too. The girls whispered something in each other's ear then Rachel said, "Well thank you boys very much." then she giggled and winked at her sister. Then in a serious voice with a straight face said, "But you don't think they show too much skin do you boys?" Then both girls started laughing as hard as they could. At first the boys just stared at each other and then at the girls' then back at each other then they started to laugh along with the girls.

They were all still laughing when they heard voices behind them. They all turned around to see Adam Henderson standing there. Along with him were three of his buddies that were always his shadow. Adams' dad owned the hardware store over in town. Adam was a big boy; he was a good six inches taller than Brady and a good fifty pounds heavier. Because of his size he was one of those bullies that thought he could push around anyone smaller than him. His buddies got their courage in his shadow as long as they could hide behind his size.

These four boys were in for a lesson they weren't likely to forget for years to come. The first lesson that they would learn was that size really doesn't mean a whole lot if you don't know what to do with it. The next thing they would learn was the difference between city boys and rawhide tough ranch boys.

Brady said, "Howdy boys", in his usual friendly manor. Adam stepped up and said, "What are you doing talking to my girlfriend you dirt ranching trash?" Rachel said, "You get on and mind your own business Adam Henderson. I never could stand your looks or your smell." Then both girls laughed out loud and Brady and Chance giggled a little too at the way Adam turned beet red and was madder than a hornet that had been swatted at.

Then Adam made the mistake of calling Rachel a tramp and poking Brady in the chest with his finger and asking him what he thought was so damned, he never got the word funny out because Brady came up with a punch that caught him right under the chin and set him right on his butt. Two of his buddies stepped forward and one of them started to say something. He barely got his mouth open before Chance threw a right then a left and set both of them on the ground next to Adam. The fourth boy was a little smarter than his buddies because he stepped back and raised his hands and shook his head saying he didn't want any of this.

Brady reached down and picked up Adam by his collar like he didn't weigh any more than a feather and said, "I think you owe these girls an apology." Adam said, "I don't owe anybody a damned", that's when Brady punched him in the gut. When he doubled over Chance came up from the ground with a punch that brought Adam clean off the ground and he landed flat on his back out cold. Adam's buddies quietly picked him up and carried him off.

Then the Walker boys and the Wilson girls went over to visit with Thelma. After a little while the boys reluctantly went with the girls to meet their parents. When they got over to where the Wilsons were sitting their dad was there talking to Mr. Wilson. They heard their dad tell Mr. Wilson, "Yea I guess your right Mr. Wilson, It's about time I got me one of them new tractors and a truck if I am to keep up with the times." The boys looked at each other with a look of total surprise. Then they both grinned from ear to ear.

3

After Uncle Hank had his fill of fried chicken and biscuits he went off to find Reverend Hatcher and his bottle of whiskey. Biscuits gave him a mighty powerful thirst. Truth be told, just about anything gave him a powerful thirst. He found the good Reverend out behind the church. From the looks of him he had gotten a head start on Hanks bottle of "Holy Water".

The Reverend handed Hank his bottle of whiskey and said, "Have a drink old friend." Hank took the bottle and said, "Here's to you Reverend Hatcher." The Reverend said, "Please just call me Hatch, that's my drinking name to old friends." Hank said, "Well here's to your health Hatch old bubby." Then he chugged down a big drink and handed the bottle back to Hatch.

The two of them set there and talked about old times as they worked on that bottle of whiskey till Lewis finally found them and said, "Come on Hank it's time to head home." After Lewis helped Hank, and the Reverend, to their feet they said their good byes and headed off to where the rest of the family waited for the long ride home.

The boys had already said their good byes to the girls with promises to see each other again. Thelma had traded a couple recipes with Mrs. Wilson and Lewis had a whole head full of ideas to think about that he thought would be good for the future of the ranch.

It was a nice slow ride on the way home. Uncle Hank was sound asleep before they got the wagon turned around and headed back to the ranch. It seemed like everyone was talking at once, until Lewis said, "Hey boys, I seen Mr. Henderson's son Adam, and he didn't look so good. Have any idea as to what might have happened to him, and a couple of his buddies?"

There wasn't a sound for a few seconds except the clop, clop, clop, of the horses' hooves on the road. Then Brady said, "Well sir, I guess you could say that they had some shortcomings in their upbringing and manners. Me, and Chance, had to show them the error of their ways, I guess you could say." Then Lewis laughed and said, "I reckon you did at that." Then they all started laughing except Thelma who didn't approve of fighting. But she could hardly keep from smiling when she thought of how much the boys had grown up and how proud she was of them.

Brady said, "Pa, are you gunna get a tractor and a truck for the ranch?" Lewis said, "Well, I'll say that I surely got a whole passel of thinking to do on the matter. Maybe it's time I thought about the future of the ranch and how to make it better and more profitable. I think that we should sit down as a family and talk things over. After all you boys are all grown up now. You boys do a, mans' share, of the work and so you should have a, mans' share of the decision making about the future of the ranch." They rode the rest of the way with everyone lost in their own thoughts.

It had been a few weeks since that day back when the walkers had made that trip to the church. It seems that a whole different family had gone home to the Walker's ranch that afternoon. They had different and new ideas about ranching, what the future holds for each one of them, what the boys thought of girls and even Thelma was considering trying Mrs. Wilson's recipe for peach cobbler. Lewis and the boys had had several discussions about what they each thought the ranch needed for improvement. Uncle Hank well he just thought whiskey should come in bigger bottles.

The boys had seen a lot of the Wilson girls over the last few weeks. But not like they had down at Wilson's creek on that one particular day. It's true that the Wilson girls were a couple of fun loving girls but that day at the creek was the only time they had pulled a stunt like that and the last time they would. They really were hard working descent ranch folks just like the Walkers, they had a lot in common with the boys and that is probably why they all got along so well.

Then one Sunday evening after supper while setting around on the porch Lewis said, "Boys, it looks like the price of beef is finally on the rise a little and folks are saying that the country in slowly crawling out of the slump it has been in for these last few years. I think that this might be the time for us to get that tractor and pickup truck we have been talking about."

The boys eyes lit up and they both said, at the same time, "Do you really mean it pa?" Then Brady said, "But won't that cost a lot of money?" Chance said, "Yea pa, where we gunna get the money, we all know you don't like to borrow money from the bank?" Lewis said, "Well I never said anything about borrowing no money from the bank. We got what, about four hundred head of cattle?" Uncle Hank said, without looking up, "We got three hundred and eighty seven to be exact. With about twenty five, ready to drop calves."

Lewis said, "Well that's close enough. I figured we could sell off fifty head with the price of beef back up. We could get maybe forty dollars a head. That would give us about two thousand dollars and that should be enough with maybe a little left over. So what do you think Hank, boys?" The boys said, "Yea that sounds like a good idea pa." Old Uncle Hank just smiled and said, "Does that mean that I get me a bottle of whiskey if there's any extry money?" Lewis said, "Well of course Uncle Hank, of course". After a few more minutes of family discussion everyone went off to bed. Uncle Hank set there by himself for a while thinking how the future sure did look like it was gunna cost a lot of money. Then he laughed to himself and thought, well he would have to see what he could do about that. Then he went off to bed as well.

The next morning Lewis headed off to town to talk to some people about the price of tractors, trucks, hay bailers, the price of beef and a few other things that might be needed to get the Walkers all "fancyfied", as Uncle Hank called it. But in reality the Walkers were a good twenty years behind the times. Lewis always went by the saying, "If it ain't broke don't fix it." But deep down inside he hoped that his stubbornness hadn't dug a hole that they couldn't climb out of. For his boy's sake he hoped not.

That same morning Brady, Chance and Uncle Hank packed up a couple days' worth of supplies on a pack horse then saddled up a couple horses while Uncle Hank saddled up his old mule Gypsy. He had had Gypsy since before the boys were born and would never ride any other animal.

Thelma came out on the porch with a bag of vittles for the boys and Uncle Hank. As she handed the bag to Uncle Hank he asked, "You got some of them buttermilk biscuits in there?" With a big smile, she said, "Why of course Uncle Hank, bout three dozen, one for the boys and two for you." Then she grabbed his face and gave him a big ole kiss right on the mouth. You would have thought she poured castor oil down his throat the way he coughed and spit and fussed as he headed for his mule. But Thelma just laughed because she knew it was just a big show. She couldn't see his big toothless grin as he walked away but she knew it was there.

After they were all packed and saddled up, Thelma told Uncle Hank to keep an eye out for her boys even though it had been the other way around these past few years. After all he was going on ninety four. Uncle Hank said, "Come on boys lets go find us fifty head of cattle." Thelma waved at the three of them as they rode off. She was thinking about what this day meant to all of them and their future. She was worried, but at the same time excited.

Lewis had spent a big part of the day talking to a lot of people all over town. He even went by the bank to see what the ranch was worth. He didn't want to waste a lot of money on the ranch if land values were so low that he would be throwing away good money and a lot of hard work that it would take to make all the changes that he and the boys wanted to do. But the banker assured him that the ranch was well worth spending money and time on. He even told Lewis that he could make a loan on the ranch if he needed to. Lewis said thanks just the same but he was going to do this without borrowing money or not at all. He thanked the banker and left.

By the end of the day Lewis had a pretty good idea as to what the improvements would cost. He figured six hundred for a good used tractor, eight hundred for a hay bailer, three hundred for a four or five year old truck and some left over for gas and oil and a bottle of whiskey for Uncle Hank. He couldn't help but laugh at this. He hoped no one seen him laughing to himself and think he was a little touched in the head or something.

One more stop at Henderson's hardware store and off to the ranch he went. On the way home he had a lot to think about. What kind of tractor should he buy, how much land should he plow under, is he gunna need a new barn and a whole bunch of other things that other people had brought up that he hadn't thought of. He hoped he wouldn't let his boys down. They were so excited about the future. He would do his best and hope for the best. That's all he could do. On the way home he couldn't help but wonder if it took three hours to get to town in a horse drawn wagon how long would it take to get to town in one of them, Automobiles.

4

Uncle Hank and the boys set up camp on the outside of a box canyon so as to have a place to keep the herd until they were ready to drive them back to the ranch. The first day the boys were able to roundup thirty-two head. They felt confident that they could get the rest in one more day. When they got back to camp that afternoon they found a fire with a pot of beans cooking over it but no Uncle Hank. They figured he had wondered off to shoot some game for their supper. It was almost dark and he should have been back to camp by now. Worried, they set off to find him. After about half an hour they found him leaning against a tree by a small stream.

He told them that he had heard an old gobbler down by the creek and figured on shooting it for supper. But as he rode up to the creek a rattler spooked Gypsy and she jumped, throwing him off. His shotgun had fallen in the creek and that's why he hadn't fired a shot in the air to tell them where he was. He said that he thought his leg was broken. Brady knelt down and took a look at his leg. He gently raised his pants leg and there was a big nasty gash about four inches long where you could see the bone. It was definitely broken by the way the bone looked out of place some. By the looks of the ground he had bled out a lot and was lucky to still be alive. Chance could see the worry in his brothers' face and didn't have to be told how serious Uncle Hank was.

Uncle Hank just laughed and said that the worst part was that his whiskey was on that damned mule and he couldn't reach it. Gypsy had calmed down after getting spooked and had settled down no more than ten feet from her old friend. After all he was the only man who had ever ridden her and he had always been as gentle to her as she had been to him. They had been companions for a life time after all.

Brady cleaned up the wound and covered the cut as best as he could while Chance found a couple sticks to make a splint out of. After they got his leg wrapped up and stabilized, the boys, one on each side, gently picked him up and set him on Gypsy's back for the trip back to camp. Brady thought he saw a tear in his little brother's eye. That just made the lump in his throat even bigger. He couldn't remember Uncle Hank ever being hurt or even sick for as long as he could remember.

They headed back to camp with Uncle Hank fussing and complaining all the way. Of course the more whiskey he drank the louder he got. The only thing was that he and the boys didn't realize that the whiskey was making his blood thinner and that made the bleeding worse. The fact that he was ninety-three years old wasn't in his favor either. And with Chance in the lead and Brady leading Gypsy no one noticed how much he was bleeding.

Uncle Hank had quieted down a lot by the time they had gotten back to camp. Somewhere along the way he had dropped, or thrown away, his whiskey bottle. He was barley awake when they lifted him off the mule and laid him down by the fire. He closed his eyes as soon as his head hit the blanket. Then they noticed that the bleeding had gotten worse on the way back to camp because there was blood all over Gypsies side.

Brady cleaned the wound again and put a clean dressing on it. He told Chance that he would stay with Uncle Hank and for him to ride back to the ranch come first light to get the wagon. Brady said that if they tried to put him on that mule again he would bleed to death. With tears in his eyes Chance said, "Brady, I been riding this range since I was five years old and I can find the ranch with a blindfold on." I'm leaving right now and I'll be back by morning with the wagon". Brady couldn't tell his little brother no and said to take his horse in case his got tired.

The next morning before the sun was all the way up Chance got back with the wagon and their dad. Lewis knelt down next to his old friend to see how he was. Brady said that he hadn't woke or moved since he went to sleep shortly after they got him back to camp last night. Lewis just nodded his head and didn't look up at first. He didn't want the boys to see the worry on his face. Uncle Hank was pale from the loss of blood and his pulse was weak. His breathing was weak too. Lewis knew that Hank might not ever wake up again. They gently loaded him in the wagon and made him as comfortable as possible. Lewis said, "Boys you did good". Then he slapped the horses' rear with the reigns and they headed for home.

The night before, Chance had come riding up to the ranch with two worn out horses and the news of Uncle Hank's accident, while Lewis and Chance hitched up the team to the wagon Thelma saddled up a horse for herself and as the men headed off to get Uncle Hank she rode to town to fetch Doc Ainsworth.

It was around noon when the wagon rolled into the yard. The doc was standing on the porch with Thelma. He stepped down the steps and up to the wagon before it even stopped all the way. He reached over the side and felt Hanks pulse. Then he said, "Ok Lewis you and the boys bring him into the kitchen and lay him on the table". From what he had heard from Thelma's description of what Chance had told her about the wound and being able to see bone, he was pretty sure he would have to do surgery as soon as possible. Thelma and the doc had gotten the kitchen ready for surgery and brought Uncle Hank's bed into the kitchen from the bunk house. Thelma had the kitchen spotless and the bed had fresh clean linen on it. Needless to say she hadn't slept a wink all night. She had food and a pot of coffee ready.

The doc cut the pants leg away from the wound to get a better look at it. After he had taken a good look at the leg he ran everyone out of the kitchen except Thelma. As they got to the door Lewis said, "But won't you need someone to help hold him down while you operate doc?" The doc said, "Trust me Lewis, he won't feel a thing". Then the doc walked over to Lewis and in a voice no one else could hear, said, "He's pretty weak Lewis and with his age it doesn't look good". Lewis said, "I know doc, just do your best." The doc said, "That you can be sure of. Now wait outside and I'll call you if I need you".

Three hours later Doc Ainsworth walked out onto the porch rolling down his sleeves as he did. He lit up his pipe as he walked over to where Lewis and the boys were waiting. He stopped in front of them then took a bid draw from his pipe and slowly blew the smoke out. He said, "He's resting pretty good right now and you boys can go on inside and see him if you want." He wanted to send the boys off so he could talk to their dad.

After the boys were in the house Lewis looked at the doc and said, "He ain't gunna make it is he doc? Is that why you sent the boys off so you could tell me?" The doc took another big draw from his pipe then put his hand on Lewis's shoulder and turned him around so they could walk out in the yard and talk without being heard.

After they got out away from the house the doc stopped, with his hand still on Lewis's shoulder he said, "It's a miracle you even got him home. If he does make it through the night, which doesn't look good, there's the possibility that he's gunna lose that leg and hell that alone would probably kill someone his age. I'm sorry Lewis I really am. We'll just have to pray that he makes it through the night and his leg doesn't get an infection". Lewis said, "Well he's a pretty tough old hombre Doc, let's not bury him yet". Doc said, "I truly hope you right Lewis", and they went back in the house.

The next morning, Thelma brought out a cup of coffee to the doc who was asleep on the porch swing. As he rubbed the sleep out of his eyes and took the cup of coffee from Thelma, he asked her if Hank had woken up yet. She said that he hadn't woken up yet but that he seemed to be breathing better. The doc stood up took a sip of coffee and smiled at Thelma and said, "That's one mighty fine cup of coffee Thelma." He thanked her for the coffee and went on in to check on Hank. She followed him on in the house to get started on some breakfast. Everyone needed to eat whether they wanted to or not.

Doc took a good long look at Hank. He changed the dressing on his leg and was surprised that there wasn't any sign of infection considering how bad the break was with so much bone showing. His color was better and his pulse seemed a little stronger to. He picked up his cup of coffee as Lewis walked up and ask how he was doing. The doc looked up at Lewis then back down at Hank and said, "Tough old Hombre, tough indeed. Well he's made it through the worst of it. The next twenty four hours should be the turning point one way or the other." Thelma had walked up and took Lewis's hand as the doc was talking.

After the doc was through talking to Lewis and Thelma about what to expect for the next few hours he said he had better head back to town. Thelma gave her husband's hand a little squeeze then turned to go back to her cooking. As she turned away she said, "Doc Ainsworth, you ain't going anywhere till you set down and have some breakfast with us." Doc, he just smiled, set down and dug in. After breakfast and about six cups of coffee the doc said he would come by in a couple days to check on Hank. But if he got worse to come get him right away. He told everyone good bye then Lewis walked him to his car.

As Doc Ainsworth got into his, nineteen-thirty-one Ford, Lewis told him thanks again and said he would come into town in a couple days to settle up on the bill. They shook hands and the doc started to leave when Lewis said,

"Hey Doc, one more thing if you don't mind before you go". Doc said, "Well of course Lewis what is it?" Lewis leaned over to doc's car and asked the doc, "Just how long did it take you to get out here from town in this car of yours?" Doc, he just laughed a little then said, "About half an hour is all Lewis." Then he headed back to town. Lewis turned around to go back in the house shaking his head and mumbling. Lord have mercy, he said to himself, "Eighteen miles in half an hour, Lord have mercy".

Early the next morning, after checking on Uncle Hank and eating a quick breakfast, the boys headed back out to round up the rest of the cows they needed and then bring the whole herd in to the ranch. The man that owned the stockyard was coming the next day to look them over. It only took half a day to round up the eighteen they needed to make up the fifty and head back to the ranch house. They got in right at sundown with a tired herd. They had pushed them a little harder than they should have but they were both worried if Uncle Hank was gunna pull through or not.

While the boys were out getting the herd in that day Thelma had kept a close watch on Uncle Hank. He was still sleeping and hadn't so much as moved a toe all day. He was breathing easy and there didn't seem to be any infection in his leg the last time she changed his dressings. Thelma was dead tired because she hadn't slept a wink since they brought Uncle Hank in. And she had not slowed down on taking care of the rest of the family. She had food ready for when her boys came home. She even had an apple pie in the oven. Mostly she kept busy so as not to worry too much.

5

THE NEXT MORNING WHILE they were all having a quiet breakfast they heard Uncle Hank moaning and moving around a little. They had moved his bed from the kitchen to the back room so it would be a little quieter but still close enough that he could be heard easy enough. They all looked at each other with excitement in their eyes and they all started to get up at the same time. Thelma held up her hand and motioned for them all to sit back down. The three of them sat back down while she went to check on him.

She went to his bed and put her hand on his chest to see how his heart beat felt and how he was breathing was. When she did he opened his eyes a little and said something in a weak voice, she had to put her ear next to his mouth to hear what he said. Then she put her hand over her mouth, stood up, and walked over and stood in the doorway to the kitchen where the others were waiting. She stood there in the doorway with tears running down her face. Lewis and the boys jumped up from the table and rushed over to her. Lewis gently took her hand away from her mouth and held it in both of his and said, "What is it, what's wrong?" Then with a trembling voice and a shaky bottom lip she said, "Biscuits, he wants biscuits."

They were all laughing and crying at the same time, jumping up and down celebrating, hugging each other and slapping each other on the back when they heard Uncle Hank say something. They all rushed to his bed and Thelma, as she sat down by his side, said, "What did you say you old Billy goat?" He gave her a weak little toothless grin and said, "What's a feller got to do around here to get some dad burn biscuits, cook em himself?" They all laughed and then Thelma stood up and with a big smile said, "Well I reckon I might be able to rustle up a biscuit or two before you break your other fool leg." Then she bent down and gave him a gentle kiss on the forehead. Then, wiping the tears from her eyes with her apron, she went back to the kitchen while the others fussed over him.

A few minutes later she came back in the room with a bowl of soup and ran everybody out of the room so she could feed him. After she gave him a bite of soup he swallowed it and made a funny face and said, "That don't taste like no biscuit to me." She just smiled at him then poked another spoon full in his mouth. She told him that if he ate all his soup she would let him have some biscuits for supper and maybe a piece of apple pie if he was good. He grinned and said, "You got a deal."

After he ate the last of the soup, Thelma got up and started for the kitchen. But before she got to the door Uncle Hank said, "Thelma, just a minute please". She stopped and turned around to look at him and waited to see what he wanted to say. After a moment or two of clearing his throat and trying to say what was on his mind he finally said, "You all know I never had me no kids, and well, if I had ever had me a daughter, I would, well, I would have wanted her to be just like you." She gave him a big smile and said, "I love you too Uncle Hank." Then she turned around and went back in the kitchen. Tears came again as she did.

Uncle Hank laid back to rest. The eating of the soup and the excitement from the family fussing over him had worn him out. He laid there awake for a little while thinking over the years with the Walker family. He wondered how an old coot like himself could ever deserve such a great family. He also wondered what he could do to help them out as much as they had him. After all he owed them everything. He even owed them two boys his life. He pondered over things for a little while and then sleep took over and he was out like a light.

It was just before noon when Mr. Ramirez, the man that owned the stock yard, drove up to the ranch. He had a couple of his hired hands with him to help look over the herd. Lewis and the boys had heard the truck pull up to the house and they all went out to meet them. After howdys were said they all walked over to the pen where the cattle were. Mr. Ramirez's men climbed into the pen and walked around so as to make the cattle move around so Mr. Ramirez could get a good look at the whole herd.

After a few Minutes Mr. Ramirez waved for his men to come out of the pen. It was quiet for a little bit while Mr. Ramirez was scratching his jaw and thinking about what he could offer Lewis for the cattle. Then he jumped down from where he had been sitting on the top rail of the corral. Mr. Ramirez said, "Now Lewis you know the price of beef ain't what it was a couple years ago." Lewis felt like he had been punched in the gut. He looked over at his boys and he could tell that they felt the same way. Lewis took a deep breath and tried not to sound too nervous and said, "Well what's the best you can do Mr. Ramirez?" Mr. Ramirez put his arms over the top rail of the fence and studied the herd a little more. Then, after a painfully long pause, said, "I'm sorry Lewis, another punch in the gut, but I can't give you any more than forty-two a head."

Lewis looked over at his boys and he could tell that he wasn't the only one that had been holding his breath. The three of them took a deep breath and looked at each other trying not to smile. Lewis said, "Well boys what do you think?" Brady cleared his throat and tried not to sound too excited and said, "Well I guess that's a fair enough price if Mr. Ramirez says that's the best he can do. What about you little brother what do you think?" Chance, in a voice that was a whole lot deeper than his real voice, said, "Well I reckon that's a fair price too Pa." Trying not to grin at his two boys Lewis turned to Mr. Ramirez and stuck out his hand and said, "I guess we got us a deal Mr. Ramirez."

Mr. Ramirez shook hands with the three of them then said he would send some trucks out first thing in the morning to load the cattle up if that was ok. Lewis said that would be just fine. Mr. Ramirez shook their hands again and he and his men headed back to town. As the truck was leaving the three of them walked back to the house to tell Thelma the good news of the sale and the price they had gotten for the cattle from Mr. Ramirez.

As they walked up the steps to the porch, to where Thelma had come out to when she heard the truck leave, they all three had their heads hanging down like things hadn't gone well with Mr. Ramirez. With a worried look on her face Thelma said, "What's the matter Lewis, boys, didn't Mr. Ramirez give us the forty a head we were hoping for?" Lewis slowly raised his head, trying to keep a straight face, and said, "No Ma, he only offered us, looking back down at the ground, Forty-Two. Then he looked up with a big grin.

Then all three of them hugged her at the same time. After the hootin, and hollerin, and dancing around on the porch, Thelma chased them all off the porch with the towel that she had been drying her hands with. She said, "I should throw that apple pie that I made this morning out to the hogs for a stunt like you three just pulled." Then she stomped back off into the house shaking her head. But it was hard to be mad when she was so proud of her men. She couldn't have been any happier and thankful than she was at that moment. Her big smile said it all. Her heart was happy.

Then she stuck her head back out the door and said, "You boys better come get some of this pie before I really do give it to the hogs." They all three came in and as they passed her the boys gave her a kiss on the cheek. As they passed she swatted them with her towel. Lewis came in last and gave her a kiss on the mouth then winked at her and swatted her on the butt as he walked by. She wiped her forehead with the towel because it suddenly felt a little warmer in there.

The next morning three big trucks came rolling into the yard. Mr. Ramirez came in his pickup and brought a check for the agreed price of forty-two a head for the cattle. The cattle were counted and loaded on the trucks then the three big trucks turned around and headed back to town with their heavy load of Walker beef. Mr. Ramirez thanked Lewis and the boys and headed back to town.

Lewis was holding the check out in front of him with a boy on each side. Brady said, "Pa, this is gunna let all our dreams come true." Then Chance said, "Yea Pa, I been dreaming about this day for a long time." Lewis put an arm around each of his sons and pulled them in close. Then he said, "This check is gunna make, your dreams come true boys, not mine." They both looked at their Pa with a puzzled look on their face. Then he smiled at them and hugged them a little tighter and said, "Boys, I have lived all my dreams. I've had your Ma by my side for most of forty years, through some good times and some bad times. But mostly good times, and better than most have had the way I see it. And I have two sons that a man couldn't be more proud of. Hell I even have old Uncle Hank. We've been together so long that I can hardly remember when he came into my life. No boys this about your dreams, I've lived mine."

Then the boys hugged their dad back and they both kissed him on the cheek. No words were needed, that said it all for the three of them. Then he handed them the check and said, "Go show this to your Ma, she worked for this just the same as us." The boys headed off to the house to show their Ma the check that would change all their lives forever. Lewis just stood there by himself for a few moments thinking about what this day had started for the Walker family. After the tears were dry, he went in to join his family and their happy talk of tomorrow and what it might bring.

It was getting too late in the day to go to town and deposit the check in the bank. And it was Friday on top of that. Lewis said he would go into town on Monday to do it. And then he told the boys and their Ma that they should have a big barbecue and invite some friends over to celebrate. He winked at Thelma and said, "You boys could invite the Wilson girls if you want."

They talked about plans for a barbecue on Sunday after Church. They figured they could do the inviting tomorrow so that everyone who wanted to come would be able to bring a dish to add to the barbecue. Lewis figured they could butcher a young steer and cook it whole over the fire pit. The boys would ride into town in the morning and do the inviting. Lewis would round up a nice young steer to butcher and get the fire pit ready while the boys went to town.

After Hank's ordeal this party would be a welcome chance to relax a little and visit some old friends. It would be a good chance for Lewis to talk to some of the other ranchers again about tractors, hay bailers, what crops would be the best to plant and what kind of truck seemed to give the best service. And what they thought the future of the cattle business looked like. Thelma would have a chance to talk to other women about woman stuff. Not that she hadn't enjoyed every second of her life with the men in her life. It's just that a woman needs to talk to another woman once in a while. Uncle Hank might be feeling good enough to sit out on the porch. A little fresh air would do him good. And the boys, well you can guess where their attention would be. You can be sure that the first ones they were going to invite would be the Wilsons'.

6

EXCITEMENT WAS HIGH THE next morning at the breakfast table. Everyone was giving their ideas as to who they wanted to invite. They all agreed on Reverend Hatcher and his wife. Hank heard this and said to tell the good reverend to bring his own bottle of whiskey. They all laughed at that. They also agreed to invite Mr. Ramirez. After all he helped to make this all possible. They agreed on several more names and after the boys had finished up their breakfast they headed off to town.

The boys had run all over town and invited everyone on their list even Mr. Henderson and his wife, at the hardware store. They thought that just because their son Adam was a jerk it didn't mean that they shouldn't be invited. They had always been friendly to the Walkers. As the boys were coming down the sidewalk in front of Henderson's store, Adam seen them and ducked out the back door. The boys greeted Mr. Henderson and invited him and his wife to their barbecue. He didn't say anything but he knew why they didn't mention his son Adam in the invitation. He hadn't seen the ruckus at the church but he had heard about it from people in town. They all had said it was Adam who started the trouble. He couldn't fault a man for protecting himself against a bully like he knew his son had become. He was ashamed of his son's behavior.

The boys talked a little more with Mr. Henderson about their plans for the ranch in the future. They talked about future needs they might have for some hardware and other items that Mr. Henderson might help them with. They said good bye and that they were looking forward to seeing them at the barbecue tomorrow. Then they headed back to the stock yards where they had left their horses when they invited Mr. Ramirez to the ranch for the barbecue.

Parties' were pretty rare these days with the way the economy had taken such a beating over the last few years. Everyone they invited said they would be glad to come. The town was already buzzing with talk of the barbecue at the Walkers ranch on Sunday. Kids and grownups alike were looking forward for a chance to socialize with old friends. It was the talk of the town.

While the boys had been in the hardware store talking to Adams' dad, he had been out gathering a gang of his buddies. He still held a grudge against Brady for the whooping he had gotten on that Sunday in front of all his friends. And this would be his chance to get even. He had a bigger gang this time and it would be a lot different. Brady Walker was going to get his.

As Brady and Chance got down to where they had left their horses they weren't there. They looked at each other and look around to make sure this was the right spot. They heard someone behind them say, "What's the matter can't you jackasses, find the jackasses you rode in on?" As they turned around they saw Adam leaning against the corral where they had left their horses tied. They looked at each other and then at Adam. Chance said, "Didn't you learn anything last time Adam?" Adam said, "Yea I learnt that I don't like you or your brother or them Wilson tramps you hang around with." And today, I figure to whip you and your brother's butt real good and proper.

Brady shook his head and said, "Just give us our horse and we'll be on our way." We didn't come into town to get in a fight with you Adam. But if you say one more word about Rachel or Jeni I am going to hand your butt to you in a basket.

Adam said, "Those Wilson girls are dirt just like you and your whole family of dirt ranchers." Brady grits his teeth and says, "You not only insulted Rachel and Jeni you've insulted my family and now, I'm gunna teach you a lesson you'll grow old with Adam Henderson." Adam smiled and started walking backwards around the corner of the corral motioning for them to follow. Adam was soon going to find out just how big a mistake he had made insulting the Walker family and two girls that would probably be Walkers themselves someday as well.

This was as mad as Brady or Chance either one had ever been. Adam should have seen this and walked away. But his bruised pride was fixing to get him the whooping of a life time. More than his pride would be bruised after today. Adam just kept walking backwards and waving them on to follow.

As they came around the corner there stood Adam and about eight of his would be tough guy followers. Even the two that were with him the last time were there. They must have thought that the odds were in their favor this time.

They all stood just a little behind Adam as if that was a safe place to be.

The Walker boys never even slowed down until they were within five feet of Adam and his gang. Chance said, "Looks like a couple of you idiots didn't learn much the last time now did you?" I guess I am gunna have to do a better job of teaching this time since you seem to be such slow learners." "You can go to the Devil Chance Walker, I ain't afraid of you", one of the, would be tough guys, said. "Oh I'm glad you ain't scared, maybe you'll hang around a little longer this time. I wouldn't want you to leave before class is over now would I?" Brady and Chance both laughed out loud. This made Adam furious. His face was beet red and his hands were shaking.

Brady grinned and said, "Which ones do you want little brother?" Brady always called Chance, "Little brother", but in reality, Chance had a good three inches taller him and was a good twenty pounds heavier. Chance grinned at his brother and said, "Oh hell, you take Adam and I'll take the rest." You could have heard a pin drop as Adam and his gang looked at each other. The confident little smirks that they had just a moment ago seemed to melt and run down their faces like hot wax. The little smirks were quickly replaced with fear and uncertainty. Chance's confidence took them by surprise. They were used to people backing down from Adam by now. They had truly misjudged the Walker boys.

Brady said, "Are you sure little brother, that only leaves about what, as he counted them, eight?" Then he said, "That's not very good odds." Chance said, "You know, your right big brother maybe we should let Adam go get a few more tuff guys like the ones he has hiding behind him." The brothers laughed out loud again.

Adam was furious and as he stepped up to face Brady he said, "You gunna run your mouth all day Walker or are you gunna take what's coming to you?" He said, "Come on boys it's time to teach these dirt ranchers how to dance." And as he was saying this he threw a punch at Brady. Brady was ready and Rattle Snake quick. He ducked the punch and came across with a right that spun Adam completely around. Adam shook his head and turned around right into a left that popped his head so far back that it looked like it was on hinges on the top of his neck. He fell straight back like a falling tree and hit the ground hard.

Four of the eight tuff guys tried to rush Chance but he met them head on. He held his arms out straight to his side and charged them like a mad bull. All four of them were knocked clean off their feet. Two of them foolishly tried to get up but Chance grabbed a hand full of hair and slammed their heads together. They were out cold.

Adam slowly started to get to his feet. Chance said, "You better stay down Adam." Brady said, "You better listen to my little brother Adam because if you get up I'm gunna make you pay for it." As he slowly got to his feet he said, "I've been the laughing stock of this town ever since our last fight Brady Walker, even the girls in town laugh at me for letting someone smaller than me whip me. I've got no choice but to finish this." Then he screamed, "This ain't over till I say it's over."

After he got steady on his feet he started walking back towards Brady. Brady said, "You don't have to do this", as Adam threw a sloppy slow punch that Brady just slapped aside. Then Adam made the big mistake of trying to kick Brady in the groin. His foot hit Brady on the inside of the thigh but didn't do any real damage.

Brady was through talking. He charged Adam with his head down straight into Adam's stomach. He hit him so hard that they both went clean over Adam backwards. Brady went right over and landed on his feet. Brady spun around just as Adam got to his feet. He hit Adam with a right to the side of the head and then a left to the other side. Somehow Adam managed not to fall down. As he straightened out to face Brady, Brady hit him right dead in the nose as hard as he could. Blood flew everywhere as his knees buckled and he fell, face first to the ground.

Chance hadn't had to do anything since the four had rushed him. As it turned out there wasn't much fight in them after all. In fact, some of them hoping to avoid some of the punishment that the others had gotten, and get on the Walker boys good side, had started to taunt Adam and were laughing and making fun of him. They were turning on him like the cowards that they were.

Adam could barely move but he could hear the others laughing and taunting him. He started struggling to get to his feet. Brady said, "Stay down Adam its' over." But he wouldn't quit and kept trying to get to his feet. After he fell down twice and staggered around like he was drunk for a little while he finally got his feet steady under him. His face was a bloody mess and you could hardly tell where his nose was. He was crying now and blubbering. Then he yelled again, "It's not over till I say it's over." Then he charged Brady with the last bit of strength in his body. Brady just grabbed him and held on to him. If he hadn't of he would have collapsed.

Brady didn't have the heart to hit Adam any more. He had to admire his courage. He just held on to him as he tried to fight and get free. He said, in a low voice where only Adam could hear, "Adam, please, stop, it's over." But the taunting continued and Adam screamed and cried even louder as he fought to get out of Brady's grasp. Brady looked over at Chance who was looking as if to say it's over brother, let's go home. Brady slowly let go of Adam who almost fell when he had to rely on his own strength to stand. Brady said, "It's over Adam, we're going home." Then he and his brother turned their backs and started to walk away.

Adam screamed as loud as he could and hit Brady in the back of the head. Brady froze in his tracks, and then slowly turned around. Brady clinched his fist and took a step towards Adam. Then he stopped and looked at Adams bloody mess of a face with tears mixed in with dirt and blood. His hand relaxed as he looked over at his brother, then looked back at Adam and said, "It's over Adam." Adam screamed, and said; "It's not over till I say it's over," and then he hit Brady with all the feeble strength that he could muster. Brady saw the punch coming and went with it as if it really connected. But it was so weak that it wouldn't even leave a red mark. Brady collapsed at his brothers' feet. Chance was shocked at first. So was Adams gang, especially Adam. He just stood there on wobbly feet and looked at the fist he had hit Brady with like he didn't know where it had come from.

Chance bent down next to his brother who was facing away from Adam and his gang where only he could see his face. Chance looked at his brothers' face and his eyes were closed. Then Brady opened one eye and smiled and winked at his brother then closed his eye again pretending to be out. Chance forced the grin that was on his face away before he stood up. And in as straight a face as he could he asked Adam, "Well, is it over now?" Adam was too weak to even answer so he just shook his head as best he could that it was. Then he staggered off with a buddy under each arm to hold him up. And of course his back stabbing buddies were now telling Adam how big he was for knocking Brady out.

After they were gone, Chance said, "You can get up now big brother their gone." Chance helped his brother to his feet and they headed to their horses. As they walked to their horses Chance said, "I'm mighty proud of you big brother. You gave Adam more than he deserved, do you think he had any idea that you were faking it?" Brady said, "I doubt that he could even tell you what day of the week it is right now." All I know for sure is that it had to end and that was the best way I could see to do it. I couldn't hit him anymore. I would have been no better than him if I did." Chance said, "Well, you make a pretty good possum big brother," and they mounted up and headed home. Mr. Ramirez stepped back into his office shaking his head. He had seen it all.

7

THERE WAS A BIG crowd at church on Sunday morning. There was a lot of talk about the party at the Walkers' ranch that afternoon. Brady, Chance and Thelma were there but Lewis had stayed home to get the beef started cooking. He wanted to cook it nice and slow so it would be good and tender. Uncle Hank was still weak from his ordeal and he stayed home as well. Reverend Hatcher gave what was probably the shortest sermon he had given in years. After church was over and everyone was outside talking several more people got invited. There would be a big crowd if everyone showed up.

Thelma and the boys hadn't been home an hour before the first guest started to arrive. It seemed like the whole county was coming judging by the line of cars and trucks coming down the road. There seemed to be a line of traffic a mile long. The more the merrier thought Thelma. It had been too long since folks had had any reason to celebrate and forget their troubles for a little while and just relax and enjoy good company. It would be the first time in years that some of the folks had seen each other.

Lewis had the beef smelling mighty tasty by now. By the time they ate it would be practically falling off the bone. The boys had set up tables and chairs all around the yard. They had also set up a couple horseshoe pits off to one side of the yard. Some smaller tables were made up out of old crates for anyone who might want to play dominoes or checkers.

Thelma had biscuits in the oven, two big pots of beans on the simmer, corn on the cob on the boil over an outside fire and half a dozen pies were on one of the tables already. She even had a few jars of homemade black berry jam to go with her buttermilk biscuits if anyone wanted. She had even put a bunch of potatoes in an old Dutch oven in the fire pit for Lewis to keep an eye on. With everyone bringing their own dishes to add to what she had there should be plenty food she thought.

As the cars and trucks started to roll in, Brady and Chance would help them find a spot to park out by the barn away from the house. Thelma didn't want dust to get on the food. When the Wilson's came into the yard Brady had them park up next to the house of course so they could unload a bunch of food that they had brought to add to what Thelma had prepared. They put it on the table with what Thelma had already set out. There turned out to be so much food brought that they had to set blankets out on the ground to set it all on. No one would go home hungry this day for sure.

Besides all the cars and trucks that came there were also several young people, Brady and Chances' age and younger, who rode their horses. This was still a time and place in America that horses were still a daily part of most peoples' lives. And of course after a couple hours of bragging who had the fastest horse there was a horse race set up for everyone to watch later. These were the simple days when you could enjoy life with what you had and not be worried about keeping up with the Jones's. It was some of the hardest times in America, but at the same time when you look back, it was also, some of the simplest and best times as well.

Lewis had guessed that about thirty or forty people would be coming but as they kept on coming it was starting to look more like sixty or seventy. As Thelma walked up to his side he said, "There sure are a lot of folks here Ma." She put her head on his shoulder and said, "Yea I know, ain't it wonderful?" Lewis said, "Some of these folks I don't know." Thelma said, "Yea, there's a few I don't recognize either. I think that there are some folks who have relatives living with them who have lost their homes due to hard times over the past few years. I'm glad they're here though. People need a reason to smile and laugh once in a while even when things are hard." Lewis said, "Yea your right Ma, people need to know that life has more to it than hard times."

There was people enjoying themselves at dominoes, checkers, horseshoes and even a friendly little poker game was going with some of the older men. They were playing for matches not money. There was a guitar and a fiddle and even a banjo playing. There were a few people starting to dance a little out in the yard. After a little coaxing Rachel and Jeni even managed to get Brady and Chance to dance. After a few dances with the girls the boys both had a dance with their mom. And then they even danced with the twins. They would carry them around on the top of their boots and swing them around with them giggling and laughing out loud.

Doc Ainsworth set on the porch steps talking with Uncle Hank. He still couldn't believe the old rascal had pulled through his ordeal with his accident. Even though Uncle Hank had survived loosing so much blood and having such a badly broken leg he would never recover enough to work out on the ranch again or even ride his beloved mule Gypsy again. Uncle Hank would joke about it on the outside saying hell anybody near to a hundert years old didn't need to be riding no dad burn mangy old mule anyway. But you could see the real pain in his eyes. It was like he had lost a big part of his life.

Reverend Hatcher had brought a bottle of whiskey for his old friend Hank. But Uncle Hank just set the bottle down by his chair and said he would save it till he worked up a thirst. No one had ever heard of Uncle Hank not being ready for a drink of whiskey at the drop of a hat. The Reverend Said, "Just give me a shout old friend when you get a thirst and I'll come a running." Uncle Hank said, "You got a deal Hatch old buddy."

No one knew it at the time but Uncle Hank would never have another drink of whiskey for as long as he lived. Deep down inside he knew that the whiskey had almost cost him his life. At his age he didn't figure that would be around much longer and didn't want to rush things.

It was getting on close to sundown but only a few people had left. It was as if no one wanted the day to end. The last few hard years had made an already hard life even harder and this party had given a lot of folks something to smile and laugh about. It was the first time in a long time and they just wanted it to last as long as possible. Tomorrow would come soon enough and along with it the same hard times that everyone was able to leave at home if only for one short day. They just wanted to enjoy every moment they could.

Chance and Brady were talking and playing checkers with Rachel and Jeni down at the end of the porch. They weren't close enough to where Thelma and Lewis could hear what they were saying. They were sitting next to Uncle Hank in his rocking chair on the other end of the porch. Lewis said "Ma, what do you suppose them young uns is talking bout?" But before she could answer, Uncle Hank said, "Dreams, their talking bout their dreams, just like we all did when we was young."

Thelma put her hand on Uncle Hanks shoulder, and said, "What did you dream about when you were that age Uncle Hank?" Uncle Hank reached up and scratched his old rough face then looked at the kids again and said, "Oh I guess I had the same dreams as most did, meet a good woman, own my own spread, live to be a hundert and find Cortez's gold." Thelma and Lewis both laughed at the last part, but then Thelma asked in a serious voice, "Well did all your dreams come true?" Uncle Hank gave her a small toothless grin and said, "Yea I recon they did mostly."

Then Hank talked about some of his life that he had never talked about and they had never asked about. They had always figured that a person's past was their own business and not to pry. Fact was they found out that Hank had been married twice when he was younger and they had both died of sickness. He never had any kids and didn't have any family except the Walkers. After his second wife had passed away he just rode off from his ranch in Texas with one saddle bag of clothes and personal belongings not planning to ever look back. He said he still owned the ranch but had let a hired hand stay on as long as he wanted. He hadn't written to him in years. He had left money in the local bank to keep up with the taxes.

He left Texas and rode out to Arizona to do some prospecting and spend time alone. He said it was years before he felt the need for any company or friendship. The loss of two wives had hurt him pretty deeply. He had heard stories of Cortez's gold from some old prospectors he had shared a campfire with a time or two. He spent years looking for the gold. "I was, pretty lucky you might say, at prospecting", he said with a big grin. Then he laughed out loud and slapped his leg and said, "Mighty lucky, yes sir, mighty lucky."

Thelma and Lewis had been speechless during his whole story. Now they looked at each other as if to say they couldn't believe their ears. Uncle Hank was quiet now so Thelma finally said, "Well how did you finally come to land here at this ranch?" After Uncle Hank thought about it for a while he finally said, "Well I come across Lewis and his Pappy struggling here on this ranch and took an instant liking to the both of them. They were hard working honest men and I hadn't been around many folks for some years and thought that this was as good a place to stop wandering around as any. They gave me a job and a chance to get back among the living, so to speak. They surely didn't pay much but they got me a bottle of whiskey once in a while and treated me mighty good. My wandering days were over. Besides, I surely didn't need to prospect anymore now did I?" Then he laughed and slapped his leg a couple times then got quiet again. Thelma and Lewis just looked at each other speechless.

It was about that time that a truck with four or five boys in the back of it drove up into the yard. It was Adam Henderson and some of his gang. Brady and Chance got to their feet and Brady looked over at his brother and said, "Here we go again." Brady just shook his head as Adam and his gang came towards them. As the boys stepped down the steps of the porch to face Adam and his gang, a crowd gathered around as they came closer. Mr. Ramirez moved up close behind Brady.

Adam yelled, "Brady Walker," then walked up to within two feet of Brady and looked him right in the face. Adam had two black eyes and one was swelled almost all the way shut. He looked like he had been kicked in the face by a mule. Chance stepped forward and said, "It's over Adam." Adam said, "It's not over till I say it's over." Some of Adam's friends said, "Yea, it's not over till he says it's over." Adam looked over his shoulder and said, "Shut the hell up you cowards." Then he looked back at Brady and stepped up almost face to face.

Brady was ready to react at the first sign of trouble from Adam. He was poised like a rattler, ready to strike. Adam just slowly leaned forward and spoke in a voice that only Brady could hear, and said, "Brady Walker, I no more knocked you out yesterday than a mule can drive a car." Then he stepped back a step and stuck out his hand and said, "It's over Brady, if you would forgive me for my being such an ass and shake on it?" Brady was speechless.

Then one of Adam's buddies started running his mouth. Adam turned around and said, "If you open that pie hole of yours one more time, I'm gunna do to you what Brady did to me yesterday." He didn't make another peep. Then Adam turned back around and stuck out his hand again. Brady took his hand and they shook like two men. Mr. Ramirez was smiling now. Then Adam took his hat off and held it in front of him as he turned to face Thelma. He said, "Mam, I must apologize for interrupting your party when I wasn't invited." Then he turned to the Rachel and Jeni and said, "I want to apologize to you ladies as well for my behavior in the past."

The girls were speechless. This was an Adam that they, or anyone for that matter, had never seen. Then Adam shook hands with Brady again and then Chance. Then he put his hat back on and turned around and started to walk back to his truck. Thelma spoke up, in a stern voice, "Adam Henderson you come right back here this very minute." He stopped dead in his tracks and slowly turned around and went back to face her. He stopped in front of her, took off his hat, looked down at the ground and said, "Yes mam." Thelma stepped forward and her frown melted into a big smile as she said, "Have you and your friends had your supper yet?"

Adam looked up at her then at Brady and the others standing around then with a smile on his face and a tear in his eye, said, "No mam, Mrs. Walker, I reckon we haven't at that." Then everyone broke out into a side splitting laugh. After the laughter had finally quieted down, Thelma said, "Rachel, Jeni, would you girls please help me see to these hungry men?" Rachel said, "We would be pleased to Mrs. Walker", then Thelma took Adam by the arm and said, "Come on Adam let's get you boys some supper." Then the three ladies led them off to the food.

After they had walked off, Mr. Ramirez walked up to Brady and squeezed him lightly on the shoulder and said, "I saw that little ruckus you boys had down by my place yesterday. Adam no more knocked you out than I did. I saw you look at your brother and wink at him then pretending to be out. After the way Adam acted, he had coming what you gave him. Why did you give him a break when he sure didn't deserve it?"

Brady looked down at the ground and kicked around a couple of rocks while he thought of how to answer Mr. Ramirez. Brady looked up at Mr. Ramirez and said, "Well sir, when Adam hit me in the back of the head the way he did I just wanted to beat him to a pulp so bad I could hardly control myself. But when I looked at his face all covered with blood and tears running down his face and his own gang turning on him, I realized that I just couldn't do it. I knew that I had shamed him and took away his self-respect and pride. I didn't give him any choice but to do what he did. The way I figured it Mr. Ramirez, was that I had taken his pride away from him and I was the only one who could give it back."

Mr. Ramirez shook his head and smiled and said, "You're a good man Brady Walker and I'm mighty proud to call you my friend." Then he shook hands with Brady and said he was heading home and went to say good bye to the rest. As Mr. Ramirez said good bye and started to leave most everybody else followed his lead and started saying their good byes to. It had been a long day it had been a good day.

Adam came over and shook hands with Brady and said, "Thanks for everything." Then Adam said, with a big grin, "The next time you boys are in town I'll teach you how to drive a car." Brady smiled as they shook and said, "You got a deal friend." Adam said, "It's been a long time since anyone called me friend." He turned and walked off before Brady could see the tears creeping up on him.

The boys were saying good bye to Rachel and Jeni. Thelma, Lewis and Uncle Hank watched from the porch. Thelma said, "You know Pa, from the way those boys of ours has been carrying on with those Wilson girls I'm afraid this old house may soon come to be a little on the crowded side." Lewis said, "I think you might be right Ma." Uncle Hank said, in a matter of fact kind of way, "Your gunna need a bigger house, maybe two." Thelma and Lewis looked at each other then, at Uncle Hank. And then Lewis said, "Yea that would be one way to look at it but we don't have enough cattle to sell and build no new house."

Uncle Hank said, "I never said anything about selling no more cows now did I? Wouldn't be no dad burn ranch without any cows now would it?" Now help me out of this dad burn rocking chair and hand me my walking stick. It's time this old coon dog hit the sack." They helped him up and Thelma handed him his cane. He slowly headed off into the house. When he got to the door he stopped with one hand on the door frame to steady himself, and said, "You can't never tell, the boys might come into some inheritance one of these days real soon." Then he went on into the house grinning one of his big old toothless grins.

Thelma and Lewis studied each other's face for a moment then Lewis said, "You don't reckon that old pole cat knows something he ain't telling us do you Ma?" Thelma's eyes were open wide with a look of disbelief and said "You ain't fixin to tell me that you think that old rascal has actually found Cortez's gold now are you Lewis Walker?"

Lewis said, "Now wait just a minute, I ain't saying either way, but you got to admit that he has said some pretty crazy things lately and now this. And on top of that I have known Hank for nearly fifty years and I don't know of one single lie that he has ever told." Thelma said, "For goodness sakes, he's ninety-three years old, he's supposed to say crazy things." But deep inside, they both knew something was up with Uncle Hank. Thelma said, "Lets' forget this nonsense and go to bed."

It had been a great day for everyone. Thelma had had the time of her life with all the women folk to visit and talk to. Lewis had talked to more people than he had talked to in the last year. He had a lot of good ideas from friends about how to make the ranch work better and be more profitable. Uncle Hank had told stories to the children and had a lot of fun making them laugh. It had been a long time since small children were on the ranch. The boys had lots of fun to but mostly they talked with Rachel and Jeni.

8

EVERYONE WAS UP EARLY the next morning. This was going to be a big day for the Walker family. This would most likely be the last time that they all rode to town in the wagon as a family. The Walker ranch would soon have a pickup truck of its' own. Trips to town would no longer be a half a day ordeal. Thelma had packed a lunch for the day and of course there were some biscuits for Uncle Hank. The boys set a rocking chair in the wagon and helped Uncle Hank up into it and made him as comfortable as possible for the ride into town. Everyone was in a good mood, especially Uncle Hank it seemed. He kept grinning at Thelma and Lewis and once even winked at Thelma then laughed out loud. She was worried he was losing his mind. After they were all loaded up, Lewis said, "Well everyone today is the beginning of a new chapter in all of our lives." Then he started the wagon off to town.

They left the wagon down by Mr. Ramirez's corral and walked into town from there. They had dropped Uncle Hank off at the church to visit with his friend Hatch. Lewis headed off to the bank while the boys went down to Henderson's hardware store. Thelma wanted to just take her time and look the town over and see what kind of new stores there was in town now. She thought she might find some material to make her husband and boys a new shirt. Even Uncle Hank could use a new shirt or two she thought. And maybe, even some pretty material for a new dress for her if it wasn't too expensive. They were all to meet up at Henderson's later.

Lewis went to the bank to deposit the check from Mr. Ramirez for the cattle. He kept out one hundred dollars in cash so he could do some things he wanted to do for his family. The banker, Mr. Dobbs, told him that with all the foreclosures of ranches and farms in the area over the last few years that the bank had a pretty good surplus of farm equipment of all kinds. He was sure he could make Lewis a good deal on whatever he might need. Lewis told Mr. Dobbs that he had a few errands to do around town then he would get his boys and come back and they would look over what the bank had. Mr. Dobbs said that would be fine and he was looking forward to seeing him and his boys later.

As the boys walked into Henderson's hardware store, they were greeted by Adam and his dad. They talked about the party at the Walkers for a little while then Adam asked his dad if he could go mess around with Brady and Chance for a little while. His dad said that would be fine. As the boys started to leave Mr. Henderson asked Brady if he could talk to him alone in private for a minute before they left. Brady said sure and asked the others to wait outside for him. Adam and Chance went on outside to wait. Mr. Henderson asked Brady to have a seat as he set down at a little table by the window. Brady set down across from him and said, "Yes sir, what can I do for you?" "Oh I think you have done quite enough already Brady." Now Brady started to get a little nervous. He said, "Is this about the fight me and Adam had?" Mr. Henderson held up his hand to silence Brady. Now Brady was getting really nervous.

Then Mr. Henderson began. "I wasn't very happy with you when I saw how bad you had beaten up my son. But Mr. Ramirez came in after the fight and told me the whole story. I guess Adam had it coming after the way he treated you. And he sure didn't deserve what you did for him at the end of the fight." Brady said, "I'm really sorry Mr. Henderson." Mr. Henderson said, "You don't have anything to be sorry for Brady. You beat the tar out of the town bully and in doing so you gave me back my son."

"You did something to that boy that I have been trying to do for years but didn't know how to. Sometimes a hard lesson is the only kind of lesson that does some people any good. No Brady you didn't do anything to be sorry for at all. My son went from being a rude disrespectful lazy son, a bully to anyone smaller than him, and a lazy no good that only did enough to get by. Now he's the kind of son a man can be proud of. He's a better person today than he was yesterday. I have you, to thank for that. I'll never forget what you did for me and my son." Then Mr. Henderson stood up, with a tear in his eye, and stuck out his hand. Brady stood and took his hand and they shook. Then he went out to where the others were waiting.

Thelma had been walking around town looking in several different stores. She smiled to herself; she had never been window shopping before. There were things for sale in some of these stores that she had never seen or heard of. She saw all kinds of electric gadgets for the kitchen and house.

There was even an electric sewing machine in one store. She shook her head at that one. She could hardly believe how much the world was changing. They really were behind the times she thought.

One store had a bunch of material in the window that she thought would make some nice shirts for boys. She went in to take a better look at the material. She saw some really pretty blue material that she thought would make a nice dress for her. It was so soft and would make such a beautiful and comfortable dress she thought. She held the blue material up in front of her in front of a mirror to see what she would look like in a dress made out of it. As she was looking in the mirror at herself she notices, back across the store behind her, that there is a dress hanging that is made of the same material.

She put the material down and went over to look at the blue dress. She thought it was the most beautiful dress she had ever seen. She had never had a store bought dress before. She noticed that it was even her size. She took the dress over to a mirror to see what it would look like on her. She closed her eyes and thought of how she would look dancing in a dress like this. She was like a kid really wanting a piece of candy real bad.

But then she saw the price. Six whole dollars, which was a lot of money she thought. She took one last look at the dress then, sadly, put it back on the rack. She went back over to the stack of material and picked out two rolls of material for shirts and the roll of blue material for her a dress. When the teller told her how much it would be for all three rolls she pulled out her purse and counted her money. When she seen that she didn't have enough money for the blue material she went back and put it where she had gotten it. On the way back to the counter she took one last look at the blue dress, gently ran her fingers down the buttons on the front of it then went to the counter and paid for the two rolls of material and left the store.

Lewis had been watching her from outside the whole time. He had seen her with her back to the window as he was walking by and stepped back to watch. When he saw her stop and take one last look at that blue dress it made him sad for the times that she got by with old worn out dresses and never once complained about it. He had a lump in his throat the size of an apple it felt like. She always put herself last. As she started to turn around he went around the corner right quick before she saw him. After she had come out of the store and moved on down the sidewalk a ways, to where she couldn't see him, he went into the store she had just left.

Uncle Hank set with his buddy Hatch as they talked about the party out at the Walker's, days from the past, the future, and especially the future of the Walkers. This last subject he was most interested in. Not for himself but the Walkers. Especially the boys it seemed.

He asked the Reverend, "Hatch old buddy, if I tell you some things that no one knows but me and I don't want anyone to know till I'm planted six feet under, as a preacher you have to keep my secrets don't you?" "What in the blazes are you talking about Hank, if you want to confess your sins then maybe you had better call me Reverend Hatcher? That might be more fitting? But if you just want to take me into your confidence as one friend to another then I'll honor your wishes if that's what you want and keep your secrets."

"Oh no, I don't want to do no confessing, all though I probably should. Then he laughed a little. I just need to tell you a few things that need to be told to Lewis and Thelma and their boys after I'm gone. And I need you to do me a couple favors that need to be kept secret till I'm gone. I hate to burden you with this but you're my best and oldest friend." "Well of course Hank I'd be hurt if you went to anyone else. But I don't like all this talk about dying I tell you right now. What do you need me to do old friend?" "Well the first thing I need is a paper and pen. The second thing I need is for you to give this to Lewis on the day they plant me." Then he pulled a big thick envelope out of his coat pocket and handed it to him. Hatch took the envelope and agreed to do as asked. Hank wrote something on a piece of paper studied it for a couple seconds then signed his name to it and handed it to Hatch. Hank said "I need you to read this then sign it as a witness."

After Hatch read the letter in his hand he looked at his old friend and said, "You are quiet a man old friend. Does anyone know about this but me?" "Not a soul, just you Hatch." Hatch said, "Why now, after all these years, this could have done a whole lot of good a long time ago?" Hank smiled at his old friend and said, "Have you ever known a harder working honest family than the Walkers, have you ever known a family that was as rich as the Walkers in the important things in life, or have you ever met a finer couple than Lewis and Thelma, or a better pair of boys than Brady and Chance?"

Hatch said, "I have to agree with you old friend the Walkers are a fine family for sure." Hank said, "Well I didn't want to change the way they were. They have been my family since before Lewis and Thelma got married. I've known a lot of people in my life that this would change. I didn't want them to change. I guess you could say I was being selfish. I know now that this would never have changed them at all. And I think that now, with the boys being older and with all the plans they all have for the ranch that this is the time for me to do this."

Hank said, "I need you to give this letter you witnessed for me to Mr. Dobbs at the bank for safe keeping. I've had a good life Hatch and longer than most. We both know I'm getting close to the end of my trail." Hatch smiled at his old friend and said, "It would be an honor to carry out your last wishes."

9

MEANWHILE ADAM HAD DRIVEN Brady and Chance out to the country in his family's car, a 1931 Ford with a powerful flat-head V-8 engine, and was showing them how to shift the gears, work the foot pedals and all the basics of operating a car. After half an hour of instructions he stopped the car and put it in neutral. Then he said, "Who's first?" As Adam got out Brady slid over behind the wheel. After Adam got back in on the passenger side he said, "Now push the clutch in. No not that one the other one. No not that one either that's the gas. It's the one on the left." Brady wiped the sweat off his face with his shirt sleeve then pushed the clutch pedal to the floor. Adam said, "Good, now put it in first gear." And after quite a bit of grinding Brady finally got it in first gear. His leg was starting to shake by now. Adam said, "Now slowly let out the clutch and give it a little gas at the same time."

Brady must not of heard the, a little gas, or the, slowly on the clutch parts because as he started to let the clutch out he couldn't control his shaking legs and let the clutch out all the way real fast and pushed the gas all the way to the floor. The car lurched forward and started hopping up and down like a giant frog. Up and down, back and forth, up and down, back and forth. The car is jumping so hard that Chance is bouncing off the roof in the back seat. Adam is bouncing around and laughing so much that he can't tell Brady what to do to get the car to settle down. Adam is finally able to reach over and pull the choke out and make the car stall.

When the car finally rolls to a stop, Brady jumps out, and says, "Holy Catfish is it supposed to do that?" Brady hears Adam and Chance laughing but he can't see anyone. He walks around to the other side of the car and there's Adam rolling around on the ground laughing so hard that tears are running down his face.

He doesn't see Chance but he can still hear a muffled kind of a laugh. He looks in the back of the car and there he is upside down with his head in the floorboard. He is laughing so hard that he can't get himself out of the floor where he is stuck. Brady helps him out of the floor and gets him out of the car where he sets down by Adam. It takes a while for Adam and Chance to stop laughing and catch their breath. When they finally do stop laughing they look at each other and then at Brady and start laughing all over again.

At first Brady is mad because they are laughing at him but then he looks at all little scratches and blood on them from bouncing around in the car and starts to laugh himself. It must have taken the boys half an hour to get their selves under control and settled down. Adam and Chance cleaned their faces up the best they could. Then Chance said, "My turn," and they all jumped back in the car to give Chance his turn at driving. He took to driving like a fish to water.

After about an hour of driving lessons they headed back to town because the boys had to meet up with their dad.

Lewis was waiting for the boys when they got back to the store. He had been talking to Mr. Henderson and looking at some tools and hardware. He also looked at oil and gas cans that they would need once there was machinery on the ranch. When the boys walked into the store Lewis and Mr. Henderson said at the same time, "Have you boys been fighting again?" The boys started laughing and then Adam said, "No sir, Brady's been driving." After they quit laughing Adam told them the story of Brady's driving and the car jumping like some giant frog or something. He explained to them how they got so scratched up from bouncing around in the car. They all had a good laugh.

After a few minutes, Lewis said, "We had better go find your mom boys and have some lunch before Uncle Hank eats all the biscuits." He sent the boys off to find their mom. He told them to meet him at the church. He didn't tell them that he had to stop by and pick up a package from the store that Thelma had bought the material at.

Lewis stuck the package he had under the seat of the wagon before he drove the wagon down to the church to meet up with his family. They were all sitting under a tree out in front of the church when he got there. The boys had carried Uncle Hank, chair and all, out to the tree. They had already had lunch so Lewis grabbed a piece of chicken and a biscuit and started eating. While he ate, the boys told their mom the story of their driving Lessons. Thelma laughed till she cried. Even Uncle Hank laughed a little even though he seemed preoccupied with something on his mind.

After lunch Lewis and the boys headed to the bank to meet up with Mr. Dobbs at the bank. Thelma said that she was tired from walking and that she would set with Uncle Hank while they took care of business. She was really worried about Uncle Hank because had only eaten one piece of chicken and half of a biscuit. She thought maybe it was the heat. She hoped that was all it was. But deep in her heart she was worried that he was slowly starting to give up on life. He hadn't been himself since his accident.

The men meet up with Mr. Dobbs and they all went out behind the bank to a big fenced in lot where the bank had a bunch of farm equipment, trucks and cars stored. The bank had quite a big selection of stuff. It had acquired most of it from foreclosures during the last few years of hard times. Usually the bank would have public auctions to sell this stuff off but lately there wasn't anyone with enough money to bid on anything anyway. This would work out to be a good thing though for the Walkers. The bank needed to sell all it could and Mr. Dobbs would make them a good deal on what they bought.

After about an hour of looking at tractors, hay bailers, bull dozers, pickup trucks and all sorts of equipment, Lewis and the boys had made a few choices. They had decided on a nineteen-twenty-six Fordson tractor for five hundred and fifty dollars. Lewis had heard from other farmers and ranchers that these tractors were tuff and reliable. Even though they had the nick name "Widow Maker." This was because they didn't have rear fenders and you had to be careful not to fall off and get ran over.

Lewis let the boys pick out a pickup truck that they liked. He knew that they would be doing most of the driving anyway. They agreed on a nineteen-twenty-eight Ford. Even though it was a few years old it had less than a thousand miles on it. Of course it was black, like most everything was back then. They got the pickup for three hundred dollars. Next they picked out an older Caterpillar bulldozer. It looked well maintained and the hours were pretty low on it. This they would use it to clear off some land so they could put in some new crops. It was six hundred dollars.

Lewis was pleased with the deals that he had made with Mr. Dobbs for the pickup and farm equipment. So he went into the bank to do the paper work. The boys drove off in the Walkers new truck. Of course Chance was driving, because Brady needed a few more driving lessons. The boys drove to Henderson's Hardware store to show Adam their new truck and to load up some supplies that was waiting for them.

They all met back at the church at five o'clock like they had agreed on. Lewis and Thelma were waiting under the tree with Reverend Hatcher and Uncle Hank. The boys loaded Uncle Hank back in the wagon as Thelma loaded up what few things she had bought. She didn't notice the package under the seat. The boys said they would meet them back at the ranch. Lewis gave Brady a five dollar bill and said, "You might need to fill the truck up with gas first, and keep the change." Brady took the five dollars and the boys started to leave. Lewis said, "Hold on boys just a minute there's something that I want to give you."

The boys walked back over to their dad as he pulled something out of his pocket. He pulled out Fifty dollars and gave them twenty-five each. The boys were in shock. They had never even seen twenty five dollars and all of a sudden they have that much a piece. After a little bit Brady finally said, "What's this for Pa?" Lewis said, "Because you earned it boys, just because you earned it. Now why don't you boys go show Rachel and Jeni your new truck? And while you're at it, why don't you boys invite them to a night on the town?"

The boys hugged their pa and their ma and they even hugged Uncle Hank. You would have thought they had done something bad to him the way he fussed and complained. But everybody knew he really loved it. The boys drove off like two kids with a new toy. They were all smiles. Thelma put her arm around Lewis, and said, "You are a good man Lewis Walker, and this is the kind of things that make me love you so much."

Uncle Hank said, "I've had about all this mushy stuff I can stomach for one day. You gunna get me out of this blasted heat or leave me here to cook?" "Why, we should leave you here to cook, after all buzzards got to eat too you know", said Thelma. Then her and Lewis laughed and got in the wagon. They said good bye to the Reverend and started for home. Hatch had already said good bye to his old friend. He wondered if he would ever see him again.

It wasn't long before Uncle Hank was sound asleep in his rocking chair.

He seemed to sleep a lot these days and that worried Thelma. Lewis told Thelma about the deals they had made with Mr. Dobbs at the bank and how much everything had cost. He talked about how much more he thought it would cost to do all the things that they wanted to do on the ranch. Even though he tried to hide it she knew he was worried.

She put her head on his shoulder and held on to his arm. "I've always been happy with what we have Lewis and I've never had any dreams that you didn't help to make come true. You've been a wonderful husband, gave me two fine sons, and you even gave me old Uncle Hank here. He's always been like the father that I never knew." Uncle Hank still had his eyes closed but there was a smile on his lips and a tear in his eye that no one could see.

Lewis reached over and gave his wife a kiss on the forehead. He said, "I feel the same way, you and the boys have made me a happy man. I couldn't have dreamed of a better life than the one we have shared together. It's the boys' dreams that I worry about sometimes. I hope they can find the happiness that we have." Thelma said, "There good boys Lewis and they will do just fine." Then she said, "I think that Rachel and Jeni are gunna be a big part of their dreams. There all good kids and they'll do just fine." Lewis said, "I think your right Ma", then, he kissed her again.

10

They were quite for a little while as the horses slowly pulled the old wagon down the road headed back to the ranch. Then Lewis reached under the seat and pulled out the hidden package and laid it on her lap. She looked at the package with a blank look on her face and said, "What's this?" Lewis shrugged his shoulders like he didn't have a clue as to what was in the package. He said, "When I was looking for you earlier in town I stuck my head in one store and this lady said you had forgotten it when you left. She said it was some kind of material I think and asked me to give it to you.

Thelma held her breath and held the package up to her chest and said, "You don't think it could be that blue material I was looking at? I didn't mean to buy it I was just looking at it?" Still playing dumb, Lewis said, "Well you might as well go ahead and open it, it's a little too late to take it back so you might as well keep it now. Go ahead and open it up and let's see what it is."

Thelma held her breath as she held the package even tighter. She looked over at Lewis and said, "You don't think this could be that blue material do you? Oh Lewis it was so pretty. I really didn't mean to buy it she must have made a mistake and thought I did." "Well it's yours' now I reckon" said Lewis. Do you really mean it Lewis I didn't even pay for it? "Yea sure you can keep it, it probably only cost a quarter any way." "Oh no Lewis, it was almost a whole dollar." Lewis said, "Well you can pay for it the next time were in town. What's a dollar any way Go ahead and open it up or are you gunna just sit there and squeeze it to death?"

Thelma said, "Well if you're sure," and she laid the package down on her lap. She took a big breath and started slowly unfolding the brown paper. Then she saw the blue material, and with a big grin, said, "Oh Lewis it is the blue material." Lewis said, "Well go ahead and finish unwrapping it maybe there's enough that you could make yourself something out of it." As she took the rest of the paper off, she saw the buttons. Her eyes started to water as she realized that it was the blue dress she had looked at in the store. She held the dress up and started to cry like a baby. Danged if another smile didn't creep up on Uncle Hanks face.

Things got crazy busy the next few days on the Walker ranch. Mr. Dobbs at the bank had a big truck deliver the tractor and bulldozer. He had sent out an owners' manual for each piece of equipment. Lewis and the boys picked up pretty fast on how the equipment operated. They all took turns on the tractor and bulldozer until they could all operate them pretty good. Even though Brady had gotten pretty good at driving the pickup it was Chance who seemed to be the best at operating the bulldozer. So he was the one that would start to clear off stumps and rocks on a piece of land that they hoped to plant grain on.

Brady worked with the tractor. It was slow but seemed to have a lot of power. It would pull a plow just about as deep as you dared to put it. He would start plowing some land that was already pretty clear. Lewis had arranged for some fuel tanks to be brought out to the ranch. They would need one for gasoline and one for diesel. He also made sure that they had the basic supplies for regular maintenance of the equipment.

The days were long and hard but the boys still had the strength of youth and went to see the Wilson girls almost every night after supper. Sometimes the girls would come over and spend the day with the boys working right along beside them. They would help pick up rocks from the plowed field and help pile them around the edge of the field to make a fence like a lot of people did in those days. These weren't any city girls for sure.

Rachel and Jeni had spent a lot of time at the Walkers Ranch, and the whole family, even Uncle Hank, had grown quiet fond of them. He had made the comment one day to Thelma that he thought they were the hardest working girls he had ever seen. Then he said, "Well next to you, of course Thelma" then he laughed. "Well of course", she said and laughed. The girls had grown quiet fond of Uncle Hank too. They would sit with him sometimes for hours while the boys were out plowing in the fields. They loved to listen to him tell stories. And he did love to tell stories.

The girls had spent a lot of time with Thelma too. They would help her cook and work around the house. They were both good cooks already and would have Thelma set down and rest and let them cook dinner for the whole family some times. But when it came time for buttermilk biscuits, Uncle Hank would insist that Thelma handled that chore. The girls would laugh and say why of course, no one makes biscuits like Mrs. Walker. Thelma would tell the girls to just call her Thelma but the girls were raised to show respect to their elders and it was hard to break old habits.

The boys had made plans to go out to a restaurant with Rachel and Jeni on the following Saturday night. They planned to go to a movie after dinner. This would be only the second time that the boys had been to a picture show and they were excited about this. They had asked their mom if the girls and their family could come to supper on Sunday. Thelma said that would be fine. This would be the first time since the party that the whole Wilson family had been there and Thelma wondered what it was about. But the mother in her had a pretty good idea what it was about. After all, she was young, and in love, once herself. All though her youth had passed her love for her husband and her family was as strong as ever if not more. There wasn't a day went by that one, if not all of them, gave her heart a reason to smile.

It was Saturday afternoon and the boys were getting ready to go out on their first official date with the girls. They had both picked out their favorite shirt earlier in the week and asked their mom to iron it for them. Thelma had made both shirts for the boys. She said she would be glad to and that she would have them ready when they needed them.

When Thelma had heard about the boys going out on their first date she had gotten Lewis to drive her to town one day to pick up some things. She wanted for her boys first date to be special. She took some money that she had been saving for a rainy day. It was only thirteen dollars but she thought that it would be enough to buy what she had in mind for the boys.

Later that day when the boys came into the kitchen and asked their mom for the shirts that they had asked her to iron for them. She said, "Yea they're ready, wait right here while I get them." She came back out with two brand new, Store bought, western long sleeve shirts with pearl buttons. Hanging on each one was a new western style string tie. Lewis walked in as she handed her boys their new shirts. He walked over and stood beside her.

The boys were totally shocked and speechless. They both hugged their mom then ran off to try them on. Lewis hugged his wife and said, "Things like this make me love you all the more Mrs. Walker." She said, "Why thank you Mr. Walker you're not so bad yourself." Then he smiled at her and slapped her on the rear and walked back out to set with Uncle Hank.

She was suddenly a little warmer.

Sunday morning came around and everyone was setting around the table having breakfast. The boys were talking about the movie they had watched. It was a western. The boys said the fight scenes were pretty corny but other than that it was pretty good. The main star was some guy named Tom Mix, that none of them had ever heard of. Thelma asked them where they took the girls to eat. Brady said that they had gone to the Long Horn Steakhouse down on Main Street.

Chance said, "Yea they had the biggest T-bone steak I have ever seen. I could hardly eat it all." Brady laughed and said, "Yea right little brother, you barely had any room for those two pieces of pie you had afterwards either did you?" Everybody laughed then finished their breakfast and started getting ready for the ride into town. Thelma couldn't wait to try on her new dress. Lewis couldn't wait to see her in it. Whenever Lewis looked at his wife he still saw the eighteen year old beauty that he had married nearly twenty five years ago.

The boys were loading Uncle Hank in the wagon because he refused to ride in the truck. The way he looked at it he had made it ninety-three years without riding in one and he was too old to start now. Lewis was standing on the porch with his back to the door when Thelma walked out in her new dress. The boys seen her first and they both whistled at her. When the boys whistled Lewis turned around and whistled himself when he saw his wife standing there in her new dress.

Time almost stood still for Lewis, as his wife walked out to him. Time may have slowed down but his heart was beating a lot faster now. He took both of her hands in his and said, "You look absolutely beautiful Mrs. Walker." Then he winked at her and said, "That blue dress ain't too shabby either." She slapped him on the arm and said, "Have you no shame Mr. Walker there are children present". He leaned in close and said, "How do you think they got here Mrs. Walker?" And then he winked at her again. She covered her mouth to try and hide the giggle that slipped out. Then they all loaded up and headed to town.

The boys headed off to town in the truck ahead of their folks and Uncle Hank. They wanted to go by the Wilson ranch and pick up Rachel and Jeni. Lewis headed the wagon to town for the long slow ride to town. The ride seemed really long and slow these days after making the trip in the truck a few times. Uncle Hank drifted right off to sleep. It seemed that he slept a lot these days. He just wasn't his old self any more. He ate less did less and slept more. He just never really did recover from his accident. It seemed that the old fire in his soul just got dimmer and dimmer as the days went by.

Brady, Chance, Rachel and Jeni were standing out in front of the church talking to Reverend Hatcher when Lewis pulled the wagon into the church yard. Thelma looked at her boys and the girls talking to the Reverend and looked at her husband. Lewis said, "Yea I know Ma, it won't be long now." Uncle Hank said, "Your gunna need a bigger house," then chuckled a little to his self. Thelma said, "I think you have hit the nail on the head there Uncle Hank."

The boys came over and got Uncle Hank out of the wagon. Rachel and Jeni, one on each side of Uncle Hank, slowly walked him up the steps and into the church. Uncle Hank was enjoying it by the way he was grinning with one of his big old toothless grins spread across his face as they went in the church. The boys were on both sides of the girls, then Thelma with Lewis bringing up the rear with Uncle Hanks rocker. It was the only chair he would set in any more.

Reverend Hatcher greeted them all at the door. He was glad to see his old friend again. He had this too big a smile on his face as Thelma and Lewis came through the door. He shook hands with Lewis and then Thelma and he told her that she looked lovely in her new dress. Then he said, "That new dress might come in real handy soon don't you think?" Thelma looked at Lewis, then back at the Reverend and said; "Now what exactly is that suppose to mean Reverend Hatcher?" The Reverend stuttered a little realizing that he had said, too much, too soon. Just then the church organ started playing and he said, "You'll have to excuse me Thelma it's time for services to start now," and turned around real quick and went to the front of the church.

The Reverend rushed off to the front of the church realizing that the kids hadn't talked to their folks yet. He really didn't have to say too much anyway. Thelma wasn't blind and she could see things changing with the boys. She could read between the lines just fine. After all she was a woman and their mother. Sometimes she thought she knew more than she wanted to admit. She looked at her husband and she knew that he knew just as well as she did that wedding plans were in the future. She always knew that this day was coming. She also knew that by the way the kids have been acting lately that this day wasn't too far off either. But the mother in her would always see her boys as her babies no matter what.

With the final hymn over and everyone making their way out of the Church it was Thelma this time that had to be shaken out of the trance she was lost in. She had got totally lost in her thoughts about her boys, the Wilson girls, the future and what it all might bring. She even wondered if she would be a grandma in the near future. She got up and took her husbands' arm as they walked to the door. She was still in a daze when she shook the Reverends hand. She held on to his hand as they shook and leaned forward and said, "I knew this day was coming Reverend but I didn't know it would be so soon."

With Uncle Hank loaded up in the wagon and Thelma and Lewis ready to get in, the boys along with Rachel and Jeni came over to Thelma, Rachel took Thelma by the hand and said, "We want to thank you for inviting us and or family over for supper tonight. It will give us all a chance to visit and talk. My mom wants to talk to you about some things. This will give us", she turned around and looked at Brady, "A chance to talk." Then Rachel hugged Thelma and said they would see them about six if that was ok. Thelma said six was fine then Jeni gave Thelma a hug to. The boys hugged their mom and said they would be home after they took the girls home.

Lewis walked up and put his arm around his wife and said, "I think things are gunna get real interesting real fast around the Walker ranch Ma." Thelma just shook her head yes. She couldn't get the words past the lump in her throat. Thelma and Lewis got in the wagon with Uncle Hank and headed for home. Thelma held her husbands' arm and put her head on his shoulder. She was quiet for a while before she finally spoke. All she said was, "Lewis, I think I am gunna like having them girls in the family." Lewis said "Me too Ma, me too." Uncle Hank said, "We're gunna need a bigger house," then laughed out loud. Thelma and Lewis laughed along with him, bigger house indeed.

The rest of the trip was pretty quiet till Uncle Hank said, "By the way, I invited Hatch to dinner tonight." Thelma turned around to face Uncle Hank, and pretending to be mad, said, "Oh you did huh?" He gave her a big ole toothless grin and said, "Yea, we might have some celebrating to do after supper, and old Hatch is my drinking buddy." She smiled back at him, and said, "The more the merrier Uncle Hank." He laughed again, and said, "Like I been saying, we gunna need a bigger house." Then he laughed so hard he could barely stay in his chair.

The boys had taken the girls home after church. They had invited the girls' family to supper that morning at church but ask them if they were coming for sure. Mrs. Wilson said she wouldn't miss it for the world. She was as nervous about this whole thing that was going on with her girls and the Walker boys as their mom was. Her motherly instincts were working over time the same as Thelma's. She said she would bring a dessert for supper to go with whatever their mom had planned.

11

THELMA GOT BUSY IN the kitchen. She had Lewis butcher and clean four young fat chickens for frying. She thought that she would make a peach cobbler using Mrs. Wilsons' recipe. She thought that would make Mrs. Wilson feel at home. As she headed out to the cellar to get some canned peaches she passed Uncle Hank on the porch. As usual, he was sitting in his favorite chair. He asked her if she was gunna make some buttermilk biscuits. She said, "Well of course I am Uncle Hank, that fried chicken would hardly be fit to eat without some biscuits now wouldn't it?" He laughed and slapped his leg. He said, "You're a gal after my own heart Thelma Walker, you surely are." Then they both laughed. She bent down and gave him a kiss on the head and went back to her kitchen. Of course he fussed like he hated it, but both of them knew that he really loved the attention.

Thelma not only had fried chicken and biscuits she had mashed potatoes, brown gravy, corn on the cob, fresh green beans and boiled cabbage on the menu for supper. And besides the peach cobbler she had made a couple strawberry-rhubarb pies. This would not only be a day to remember, it would be a meal to remember.

Reverend Hatcher was the first to arrive that evening at the Walkers. He set on the porch with his old friend while everyone else was busy getting things ready for company. This would be a big day in the life of the Walkers' but no one knew just how big except Reverend Hatcher and Uncle Hank. The two of them set quietly and talked about some of the things that they had talked about at the church the last time they met. Uncle Hank had wanted his buddy there to give him a little support with some of the things he had to say later. He wanted to make sure that they believed him and that he wasn't just a crazy old man. He really didn't doubt too much that they would believe him he just wanted his friend there with him mostly.

The Wilsons showed up right at six as promised. The four girls were still in their Sunday dresses. Mrs. Wilsons' eyes showed that she had been crying. The only reason Thelma didn't look the same way is because she had kept herself busy cooking all day. And she had cooked enough food to feed a small army. The girls and their mom all went up on the porch with Thelma. They all got busy helping set the table and bring out the food. Then Thelma brought out her peach cobbler and set it down on the table. She told Mrs. Wilson that she had finally tried her recipe and she hoped it was up to her standards. Mrs. Wilson, along with Rachel and Jeni, looked at the peach cobbler then looked at each other and started laughing out loud.

Thelma looked at the three of them and couldn't believe they were laughing at her like that. She was embarrassed then she started to get a little mad at them. Mrs. Wilson saw the look on her face and put her arm around her and gave her a big hug and said, "Oh no dear we're not laughing at you." Then she told Jeni to get her the basket that they had brought, out of the car. Jeni ran out to their car and came back with a large covered basket. She handed it to her mom who set it on the table next to Thelma's cobbler. Then she opened it up and took out a peach cobbler that looked almost exactly like the one that Thelma had made. Thelma looked at the two peach cobblers sitting side by side and starting laughing along with the rest. They all laughed till they had tears in their eyes.

The boys had set up tables and chairs on the porch. It would be a little more comfortable for everyone outside than in the house. Lewis had gotten the fire pit ready for a bon fire because Uncle Hank had ask him to so he could tell stories after supper. He thought nothing of it because he knew how muck Uncle Hank loved to tell stories.

The boys were out in the yard playing with Kari and Kali giving them piggyback rides. The twins didn't have any brothers and they really had come to love the boys like big brothers. The boys never did treat them like they were in the way whenever they were visiting with their sisters. They always took time to talk to them and give them some attention when they could. The big girls were not at all jealous of the time the boys gave their little sisters because they thought that it was important that their whole family thought highly of Brady and Chance.

Lewis asked Mr. Wilson if he would walk out to the barn with him. Lewis wanted to show Mr. Wilson the tractor and talk about the plans that he and the boys had for the ranch. Mr. Wilson stopped just outside the barn. He said, "Now Lewis, just because I'm a few years your senior you don't have to call me, Mr. Wilson. Besides something in the air tells me that we are going to be seeing a lot more of each other from here on out if you know what I mean. Please just call me Will." Lewis said, "You might just have a good point there Mr. Wilson." He stuck out his hand and said, "Proud to meet you Will." They laughed a little then slapped each other on the back and went on in the barn.

Thelma asked Rachel and Jeni if they would round everybody up for supper. The girls ran out the door all smiles and giggles to tell everyone to come to the house for supper. As the girls headed out the door Thelma and Mrs. Wilson stepped out onto the porch. While they were waiting Thelma said, "Mrs. Wilson, what's it been fifteen years or so since we became neighbors?" "Closer to twenty I would think", said Mrs. Wilson. Thelma said, "Well my goodness twenty years. Twenty years and I'm ashamed to say that I don't even know what you or Mr. Wilsons' first names are. You've always been Mr. and Mrs. Wilson to me."

Mrs. Wilson laughed a little as she rubbed her chin and thought about what Thelma had said. She said, "Now to mention it, I can't remember the last time that anyone called me by anything except Mrs. Wilson. I've been calling him Wilson and him calling me ma for so long that I can't remember when we stopped using our first names, sort of sad now that I think about it. It surely would be good to hear my own name for a change." Mrs. Wilson said, "Mr. Wilson's name is Willard, and my name is Lola Marie, but you can call me Marie." Thelma said, "What a beautiful name Lola Marie is. I think we're gunna be the best of friends Marie." Marie gave Thelma a big hug and said, "I think you're right Thelma."

Everyone gathered on the porch for supper. The food was all on one table by the door. Everyone could fix their plate then sit at the table of their choice. Thelma, Lewis, Marie and Will sat at one table. Hank, Reverend Hatcher and the twins sat at another and the four grown kids sat at a table at the end of the porch. The Reverend said a prayer and they all dug in.

After a few minutes Thelma got up to see if Uncle Hank needed anything. She had put two biscuits and two pieces of chicken on his plate when she fixed it for him. He hadn't touched his chicken and had only eaten half of one biscuit. She also noticed that he was sweating a little and his breathing seemed to be a little heavy. She leaned over and asked him if he felt all right. He said it was nothing. He said it was just the excitement and his tummy felt a little jittery is all. She put a hand on his shoulder and leaned over where no one could hear her and said, "Are you sure, you don't look so good?" He assured her he was all right and she went back to her seat.

When she sat back down Lewis could see the worry in her face as she looked over at Uncle Hank. He said, "Is everything all right with Uncle Hank?" "I'm just a little worried about him is all, he has hardly touched his supper and he is sweating like its' a hundred degrees out here. He says that he is just a little excited and has an upset stomach."

Lewis squeezed her arm a little and said with a smile, "He's not the only one who is excited around here today. We're all as excited as a steer at branding time. I think he knows what the kids are up to the same as us. It's an exciting day for all of us." Marie said, "Yea Thelma, my stomach is all in knots. Why it's a wonder that any of us can eat at all." Then she looked at Will and said, "Well some people seem to be able to eat just fine", as he shoveled in a fork full of boiled cabbage. That made everyone laugh and it made Thelma feel a little better. But she was still worried about Uncle Hank.

After the laughter quieted down Lewis said to Thelma, "I'll go to town in the morning and ask Doc Ainsworth to come out and check on him as soon as he can." Thelma said, "Thank you Lewis it will make me feel better if the doc checks on him."

Trying to hide her worry and get her mind on other things she said, "Well Willard what will it be, some of my peach cobbler or some of Lola Maries' peach cobbler for dessert?" Will froze in between bites, you could have heard a pin drop, then he choked down the bite he had in his mouth and said, "Why I'll have some of both of course. I wouldn't want to offend Lola Marie or you Thelma now would I?" Then they all broke out laughing again.

Everyone was done eating at all three tables so Thelma and Marie got up and started to put up food and clean up the supper mess. Rachel and Jeni saw their moms get up and start to clean and they both went over to where they were. They told them that they would take care of the cleanup and for them to go set somewhere and relax. Brady and Chance came over and started helping the girls clean up. Brady said, "Yea mom you ladies go relax, we got this." Marie said, as they started walking away, "I truly do love those boys of yours Thelma." Thelma said," Well I feel the same way about your girls Marie."

Lewis stood up and said, "You don't have to tell me twice," and grabbed two chairs and went off the porch to find some shade. Will grabbed two more chairs and followed him. Thelma and Marie put down the dishes that they had picked up and went off to follow their husbands. The boys moved Uncle Hank, and his chair, out to where the others were sitting and the Reverend grabbed his chair and joined them. The boys went back to give the girls a hand and the twins went off to play.

It was just getting dark when Lewis went over to the fire pit to get it lit. Will started moving all the chairs over to the fire pit. The women got up and moved with them as did the twins. Uncle Hank was moved over by the fire by the boys.

It was just getting good and dark and the fire was going good. Thelma and Marie were talking to each other and so were Lewis and Will. The twins were pestering Uncle Hank, but he loved every minute of it. No one had even noticed that Brady and Rachel' and Chance and Jeni had walked up until Brady cleared his throat real loud to get every ones attention. It got totally quiet real fast. Thelma grabbed a hold of Maries hand and squeezed it. They looked at each other like they knew what was coming now. The dads glanced at each other too and looked back at Brady. Uncle Hank giggled and said, "Hot dang, here it comes." The Reverend said, "Now Hank let the man speak."

Brady cleared his throat again and began, in a somewhat shaky higher tone than usual. "The four of us have some things to say to all of you if you would please give us a few minutes. We have been doing a lot of talking and we all have something to say." He stepped aside and Rachel stepped forward. She looked back at her sister and stepped back and gently took her by the hand and pulled her forward with her. The sisters held hands as Rachel began. They weren't the only ones holding hands because Thelma couldn't let go of Maries' hand. She didn't even know she was still holding it or how hard she was squeezing it.

Her voice was a little shaky at first but as she spoke she got more confident and started to relax a little. She said, "Mom, Dad, Mr. and Mrs. Walker, It's no secret that over the past few months Brady and I and Jeni and Chance have been seeing a lot of each other." Uncle Hank, thinking about the day at Wilsons' creek, couldn't help but laugh a little. When he laughed she looked over at Brady as if to say, did you tell everyone. Brady and Chance were both looking at the ground. She composed herself and continued.

"As I was saying, she gave Uncle Hank a look that said that will be quiet enough out of you, we have been seeing a lot of each other and have been talking a lot about the future and what the four of us see the future bringing us. I think I speak for all of us when I say, that we all want the same things. And that is to share our lives with someone we love, someone with the same values, someone who isn't afraid of hard work and hard times. We all want what our parents have, she looked over at her mom and dad and smiled, and that is to go through live with someone who is willing to stand beside you through whatever life throws at you, someone to share our dreams with, someone who will love us for the rest of our lives."

Now Jeni began to speak. "I don't think there has ever been, two couples who have so much in common. We have all been raised by parents who weren't afraid to show us discipline when we needed it and were never slow at showing us love when we needed it either. You have taught us the difference between right and wrong. You have taught us when to be tuff and when to be gentle and sensitive. Dad, I don't think that I have ever heard you talk to our mom like she was anything less than your equal. These are the things we want. We want someone to show us that kind of love. She looked at Rachel and said we think we have found that in Chance and Brady."

Chance moved up next to Jeni and took her hand. Then he said, "Ma, Pa, we know that we have been making a lot of plans for the future and the things we want to do with the ranch. Now we're not saying for one minute that our plans and dreams are any different today than they were yesterday. It's just that Brady and I want for Jeni and Rachel to be part of what the future has to offer us. We want them to share our dreams, like you and mom have done your whole life. And like Jeni said I don't think you will find any two couples who have so much in common."

Brady spoke up and said, "We know this isn't the greatest timing in the world and that this will make things harder before they get easier. But like you and mom have always taught us, the important things in life are worth working for. The four of us know that there will be some sacrifices from all of us. We will all have to do our fair share. We know that there are new plans to be made and some rearranging of our lives. Brady paused and looked at Rachel and Jeni and Chance and said, are you all ready?" They all shook their heads yes. Brady said, "Well I have asked Rachel to marry me and Chance has asked Jeni to marry him." At the same time the girls shouted, "And we said yes".

Of course both moms are bawling like babies and the dads are grinning from ear to ear. Uncle Hank managed to stand and do the jig a little before he had to sit back down. The moms got up and started to come over to their kids when Chance held up his hand and said, loud enough so everyone could hear him, "Now just a minute everyone that's not all." Both moms sat back down.

Jeni said, "It's true that I did say yes when Chance asked me to marry him but we both agree that we need to wait a couple years before we get married. It's not only that we think we are still a little young but we think that it would be too hard on everyone if we all four got married at once. For one, it would be too hard on the Walker household with that many people living here all of a sudden, and second it would be unfair for the Wilson ranch to all of the sudden lose all the ranch help. So Chance and I have decided to wait a couple years. If we really love each, a little time won't matter. What's two years anyway?" No one moved a muscle. Then Jeni, after no one made any effort to get up or say anything, said, "Ok were through talking now how about some hugs over here somebody."

Thelma and Marie rushed over to their children. Hugs, kisses, crying, more hugs more kisses more crying. The men all hugged all around. Uncle Hank said, "The first one to kiss me will get this cane of mine up beside their head." Of course all four of the kids came over and gave him a kiss. Even the twins did too. Lewis hugged his boys and told them how proud he was of them. Will shook hands all around. There was hugging and kissing from the two moms for all the kids. And of course the women were all, crying now. The twins were even in the spirit of things with their own little happy dance. The Reverend went to each of the young adults and gave them his congratulations. Rachel and Jeni hugged their dad then hugged Lewis.

12

Uncle Hank told his buddy Hatch that he couldn't remember ever seeing this much crying and hugging in all his born days. Then Hank asked his friend if he would get every ones' attention for him. Hatch looked at his old friend and knew that this was the time that Hank had been waiting for. He gave his dear old friend a gentle pat on the shoulder and said, "It would be a pleasure old friend."

The Reverend walked over to where everyone could hear him. He held up his hand and said, "Folks, folks, could I please have your attention." He repeated it again, and after a couple minutes everyone started to settle down and get quiet. He said, "Would everyone please come over to the fire and find a place to sit down because my dear friend Hank would like to say a few words. Everyone quietly found a place to sit around the fire and settled down to listen to what Uncle Hank had to say. Lewis threw a few more pieces of wood on the fire before he sat down because he seriously doubted that Uncle Hank only had a few words to say. Something told him that Uncle Hank was about to say a whole mouth full.

It was quiet for a little while. The only sound was the crackling and popping of the fire as Uncle Hank thought about what he wanted to say and how he wanted to say it. He had figured that the letter that The Reverend held for him would have done his talking for him after he was gone but with the news they all got tonight about the kids getting married he had better go ahead and do his talking tonight.

That morning at church Hank had asked The Reverend to come out to the ranch tonight and to bring the letter that he was holding for him. He wanted his old friend with him on this day because it was going to be one of the most important days of his life. He had thought long and hard about what he would say to the Walkers. The more he had thought about it the more he realized that the letter would not have been the best way to say his heart felt words. Deep inside he was glad that he had the chance to talk to them all in person and not through a letter.

Finally he started to talk. His voice wasn't as strong as it used to be but that didn't seemed to be a problem because the only other sounds in the night besides him were the popping of the fire and a few night birds talking to each other. Everyone gave him their full attention.

"I want to start off with a story of a young man in his early twenties. This young man was born in West Texas and lived on a ranch with his Ma and Pa. It was a poor ranch much like this one. They didn't have much more than a roof over their heads, but they were a happy family. This fine, good looking young man, he giggled a little at the good looking part, went by the name of, Hank Henry Sterling."

Everyone looked around at each other because this was the first time that any of them had ever heard Hanks full name. Even Lewis and the Reverend had never known him by anything other than just Hank. Only Mr. Dobbs at the bank knew his full name. That was only because his whole, legal name, was needed on some paper work that the banker had done for him. Uncle Hank continued with his story after he figured everyone had enough time to digest what he had said so far. He had that little toothless grin of his on his face as he started his story again.

"Well, this Hank Henry Sterling fellow thought that he would go out on his own and do a little prospecting for gold. He paused a little for effect. I said good bye to my folks and headed off to find my fortune. I had heard stories as a kid of Cortez and all the gold he had hidden in the mountains of Colorado and in Arizona s' big canyon. I spent the better part of five years looking around in them hills and canyons but never found any gold or treasure of any kind. I decided that it was time to head back home to my folks and the ranch. I got home to an empty run down ranch. My folks had passed away to a sudden illness a couple years back and there was no one left on the ranch but one loyal old hand that did what he could do but the ranch was too much for one man.

I didn't have any brothers or sisters so I was now the owner of a ranch. I gave up on my foolish dreams of gold and treasure and settled in to make a go of the ranch my folks had left me. A year or so later I married a childhood friend by the name of Betty. Sickness took her the next year." Uncle Hank was quiet for a little while as he was lost in the pain of his past.

"Life was hard for Hank Henry Sterling, he continued, I had just about given up on life and love and my closest friend those days was a bottle of Rot Gut, until one day, I ran into a widow woman by the name of Lana. We both had lost the love of our life and we both had spent too much time alone. After a few months of getting to know each other we decided to get married. Life was good once again for Hank Henry Sterling. I had given up the bottle and I was working hard on the ranch and Lana was due to have a baby any day and I was as happy as any man can expect to be. But it seemed that life would stab me in the heart once again though. That very month I lost Lana and our baby girl in child birth. Some say that I lost my mind that day because after I buried my wife and baby I rode off with nothing but the clothes on my back not to be seen or heard of for years."

Old Hank had to stop his story here for a few minutes as he caught his breath and wiped the tears from his face. He wasn't the only one crying though, because all the women had tears rolling down their faces by now. Even the twins were crying. While Hank took a breather and rested a little Thelma went to the house to get him a glass of water. Not a word was spoken while they all waited for Uncle Hank to continue his story. And after a few minutes and a drink of water he continued.

He started his story off again but on a brighter note this time. He thought that was enough sad memories for now. He said, "Well, I guess you folks all know by now that Hank Henry Sterling is one in the same as yours truly?" He laughed and said, "I haven't told anyone my whole name except for Dobbs down at the bank in over fifty years.

When I left the ranch that day I became just plain old Hank. I wandered around in the Colorado Mountains for four or five years and then I wandered from one end of the

Grand Canyon and back for a few more years. Why I've rode on a horse, mule, jackass, and I've even rode a raft a few times down that river in the bottom of that big canyon. I've found more caves and hidden gullies and I've found places no man had ever been in but me up till then.

It was in one of these caves that I found what I thought was going to be Cortez s', big treasure." He looked over at the boys to see if they were paying attention. They were both hanging on every work he spoke. "I come across this one particular cave by accident one day when I was chasing this here Jack Rabbit that I wanted to give a personal invite to join me for supper." Everyone got a good laugh at this. "I was chasing this rabbit on foot because I didn't want to waist a bullet on one mangy ole rabbit. As I chased this rabbit he disappeared right before my eyes." Hank stopped and looked around at his audience and they were all almost on the edge of their seats. He laughed and continued his story.

"Well I couldn't believe that there rabbit could just up and vanish into thin air so I walked up closer to where I had last seen him. What I thought was part of the canyon wall turned out to be this here giant boulder that must have been a good thirty feet tall. As I looked closer I could see a small game trail going around behind this big boulder. So I followed this little trail and guess what I found behind it?"

Hank just set there for a few seconds as if he was through with his story until Brady spoke up and said, "Well, Uncle Hank, are you going to tell us what you found behind that rock or not?" Thelma and Lewis smiled at each other because they knew Hank was enjoying his fun with the boys. Hank said, "Oh yea the rock, I forgot where I was," then he winked at Thelma and Lewis and went on with his story.

"Well, when I walked around that big rock I found this big cave that you would have never known was there unless you walked around that rock like I did. This cave must have been a good twenty feet high at the entrance. That rabbits trail led right into that cave so I followed it in the cave looking for my dinner guest." He chuckled a little at this. "It was dark in that cave and there was a smell coming out of there that could melt all the ugly off a pig.

I lit a match and waited a little for my eyes to adjust to the dark and started slowly into the cave looking for that rabbit. I figured I had him now with me between him and the exit. As I turned around to look in one dark part of the cave, I saw the biggest old bear I had ever seen, sleeping in the back of the cave. I froze in my tracks. Then the match burnt my fingers and I dropped it and that cave went dark as night. I turned around and ran as fast as I could for daylight. It was dark in that cave and I ran head first right into a low part of the ceiling and knocked myself out cold."

Uncle Hank was laughing so hard he could hardly catch his breath. By now everyone was laughing along with him. Everyone was laughing and some had tears rolling down their faces. Uncle Hank was coughing and had to take a few deep breaths and take another drink of water before he could continue.

"When I woke up it was dark outside and I had blood in my eyes where I had busted the top of my head open. At first I couldn't remember where I was or what had happened. I sat up against the wall of the cave trying to let my head clear when that smell hit me, and all of a sudden, I remembered the bear. I set perfectly still and listened. There wasn't a sound at first except for my breathing."

"I made it to my feet and listened for a little while and didn't hear anything so I figured that bear must be gone. I took a chance to light another match to take a look around. I was gunna look to see if that bear was still there, when I heard something rushing towards me. I thought that bear was coming for me for sure this time, so I bolted for the exit again."

Hank started laughing so hard he could hardly continue but he finally managed to say, between laughter and tears, that he ran smack dab into the roof of the cave again. He said, "I didn't hit it as hard this time but it knocked me down to my hands and knees but not out cold like the first time."

Hank had everyone laughing again and he had to take a breather and have another drink of water to get his breath back. Lewis threw some more wood on the fire while everyone stood to stretch their legs for a spell. After a little while everyone set back down and waited for Uncle Hank to go on with his story.

"So there I was he started, down on my hands and knees in the middle of the cave's entrance when all of the sudden, he paused and looked around the fire at his captive audience, there came running out of the back of that cave, the biggest, ugliest, meanest looking, he paused again, then with as serious and scared a look as he could manage, Jack Rabbit that I had ever seen." Hank sat back real serious like and didn't say a word. He didn't crack a smile at first, then everyone looked at each other and then they all broke out laughing at once.

Hank was laughing so hard that he was wheezing and coughing and couldn't catch his breath. Thelma came to his side to check on him. After he had gotten to breathing better and was resting easier Thelma put her hand on his shoulder and said, "Uncle Hank, don't you think you have told enough stories for one night? You can finish your story another night."

Uncle Hank reached up and took one of Thelma's hands in one of his and patted it with his other and said, with a tender sad kind of smile, as he looked deep into her eyes, "No sweetie, I gotta finish this story tonight." He held her hand as they just looked at each other for a few seconds and she said, "Well if you re' sure your up to it." He assured her he was and she sat back down and everyone got quiet again.

Uncle Hank said, "You know, that rabbit jumped right over my back and kicked me in the butt on his way out of that cave. Like I told you that was one mean rabbit." He laughed a little and so did everyone else. They tried not to laugh too much, for Uncle Hanks' own good. "Well I got to my feet again, emphasizing the word again, lit another match and looked around again for that bear. I had figured out by now that that old bear was either dead or too old to move or he would have already ate me and that darn rabbit both, well by cracky that bear was as dead as a rock. That must be why the smell was so bad in the cave. My match was burning short so I made me a torch out of a dry limb from a dead bush near the cave entrance. I figured I might as well take a good look at this old bear before I leave the cave."

"Once I got that stick burning to where I could see good, I could tell that old bear was as old as the hills and had probably just died of old age. He hardly had any teeth left and his claws were worn down to almost nothing. I figured that old feller just came into this cave to die." Hank got quiet for a bit and looked all around at his friends and family. Thelma fought back the tears as she squeezed her husbands' hand.

"By now I had about all of that old bears smell as I could take so I turned to leave the cave. But as I raised the torch up a little higher to take my last look, I noticed something behind that old bear that I hadn't noticed before. I eased around behind him to get a better look at what it was.

What I found, he stopped here and looked at Brady and Chance, they were both on the edge of their seat, was an old wood and leather chest. It was about the same color as that old bear so I guess that's why I hadn't noticed it at first. I only noticed it when I saw the light reflect off of what I first thought was brass hinges. It looked like that old bear had even clawed on it some by the shape it was in."

He had every ones' undivided attention at this point especially Brady and Chance. Thelma and Lewis looked at each other and Thelma squeezed his hand even harder than she already was and put her other hand over her mouth. They were both thinking about some of Uncle Hanks' comments lately about treasure and the boys maybe getting some inheritance in the near future.

Still looking at the boys, he said, "Well, I drug that chest out to the entrance of the cave to get a better look at it. Besides, the smell of that bear was making my eyes burn and was about to make me lose my breakfast, and I didn't even get any breakfast that morning." The boys were on the edge of their seats now waiting to hear what was next.

"I could tell that chest was really old by the looks of it. I've never seen anything like it in all my born days. There was a lock on it but even being as old as it was that was one tough lock. I tried to bust it off with a rock but it was too tough. I ended up using my Bowie knife to cut away at the leather straps that held it together. I had to cut it apart one little piece at a time to see what was inside."

Uncle Hank stopped here with his story and stuck out his arms and gave a big fake yawn. Then he said, "Well folks I think it's about my bed time." Then he acted like he was going to get up out of his chair. Brady and Chance said, almost as one, "But what was in the chest Uncle Hank?"

He looked at them like he didn't have any idea as to what they were talking about. Thelma was shaking her head and grinning at Uncle Hank. The look on the boys' faces was priceless and so was Uncle Hanks' acting job thought Thelma. Lewis enjoyed Uncle Hanks' performance and was quietly laughing behind his hand. He was trying not to let the boys hear him laughing.

Uncle Hank was giggling like a silly kid when he sat back down. The boys realized that he had just pulled a joke on them. They both relaxed and sat back in their chairs and waited for him to continue the story. The girls were snickering under their breath at the boys. The boys tried not to look too embarrassed even when everyone laughed again.

"Well, I finally got that stubborn lid off of that chest to where I could see what was inside. I couldn't believe what was there. What I found, he looked around at everyone, during an extended pause for effect, was an old Conquistadors armor and helmet." The boys traded a disappointed look with each other. "But, started Uncle Hank, I scratched that armor with my Bowie knife and found out that the suit of armor was made out of solid gold.

The boys' eyes were about ready to pop out of their eye sockets and if they weren't careful someone would step on their bottom lips, at the mention of the word gold. Everyone set in silent disbelief and awe. Hank just set back in his chair with that toothless grin of his, and let everyone take in what he had just told them. After everyone had quieted down, Uncle Hank said, "You know that suit of armor was so heavy that I had to go back to that cave later with a mule to carry it out of that canyon. That was my first mule, and my Gypsy, is the last mule I ever owned. Sometimes I wonder though, who owns who? She has been better company than most people I've ever known. That is, until I found my family here on the Walker ranch." He gave Lewis and Thelma a look that said a million words.

13

After Uncle Hank took a few minutes to rest he got back to his story.

"I loaded up my treasure on that mule and headed to Flagstaff where I found a man who bought it and I put all the money in the bank. I got over ten-thousand dollars for it. My ranch was free and clear and I didn't know of anything I needed or wanted to buy. Money seems to ruin some people so I just left it in the bank in Flagstaff and the interest on it kept the taxes on my ranch in Texas paid up. That all changed though, when you folks started making plans for the future and now with you young folks wanting to get married. So the way I look at it, this is the time to spend some of that money," he said with a big grin.

Lewis said, "Uncle Hank, I've known you almost fifty years and you have never had two silver dollars to rub together, why now?" Uncle Hank said, "Well I'll tell you why now Lewis. Throughout my long life I have seen money turn good people bad or make them do things they wouldn't have done if not for the love of money and what it can buy or do. And over the years I just didn't think about the money or see any need for it. But I know in my heart that you and your family would be just as happy without it as they would be with it. Your family is already rich in the important things in life. Money can't buy what you have here in this family.

I know that money can't buy your dreams, but it can help you bring them to life. And I know that it will make life a little easier with it, so I want to do that for you and your family before I'm gone. So with all the things coming up for you and your family, I think that now, is the right time to tell you all what I have done with my money."

"I had Mr. Dobbs down at the bank send some telegraphs and have my money transferred here to his bank. Mr. Dobbs even helped me find a buyer for my ranch back in Texas. I got a good deal of money from that to. Now this next part is mostly for you boys. You know that ranch just south of here, the one where the widow Branson used to live?" Lewis said, "Yea I know the ranch. It used to be a top spread before Mr. Branson passed away." Brady said, "Yea isn't that the place that was once a horse ranch? "And doesn't that place have some of the best water in the state?" said Mr. Wilson. Uncle Hank said, "Yea, you are all three right about that ranch."

Uncle Hank grinned at everyone before he went on. "When Mr. Dobbs sold my ranch in Texas I had him buy the Branson ranch for me." Lewis and the boys couldn't believe what they were hearing. Lewis said, "You mean to tell us that you own the Branson ranch now?" Uncle Hank said, "No, I don't own the Branson ranch that is now the, "Chance Walker Ranch."

Now everyone is really confused. Hank is just grinning at the lost looks on their faces. Chances eyes are bugging out and he starts to say something but Uncle Hank held up his hand for everyone to let him speak. After everyone quiets down Uncle Hank explains what he has done.

"Now as you all know I have never had any use for any money and at my age I sure don't have any need for a ranch either. So what I have done is to sign over the deed to that ranch to Chance. I have also set up an account at the bank in Chances' name with five-thousand dollars in it to get the ranch started. And in Brady s' name, I have set up an account of five-thousand dollars as well. The way I see it, this ranch, will be his someday with him being the eldest and all. I have also had Mr. Henderson, at the hardware store order all the material to build a new barn and a house, here on this ranch, for Brady and Rachel. Everything has been paid for in full in advance.

That left me with about six thousand dollars that I had Mr. Dobbs put in your account Thelma and Lewis. Oh, and one other thing, there will be two new Ford pickups delivered here for you boys by the end of the month." Everyone started to speak at once. Uncle Hank held up both his hands until everyone quieted down. Hanks voice was getting weaker.

"Now I won't have any arguments from any of you. This is, my decision, and I won't hear another word about it. The way I look at it, I am the richest man here with what you Walkers have given me in return. I have gotten the best part of this deal by a long shot. You have all made me rich in all the good things in life, things that money could never buy. You have given me your love, your friendship, your trust and most of all you have given me a family when I didn't have one. No, if any one got the short end of the stick here it was you Walkers. All I have given you has been a grumpy old fool who drinks too much and eats too many buttermilk biscuits." Thelma started crying like a baby.

"I have felt like a part of this family from the day I got here. No one has ever judged me or pried into my past, unless I brought it up first and you have all ways, excepted me as plain old Hank or Uncle Hank as you boys have come to call me. I don't think I could have felt any more like a part of this family even if we were blood kin. Believe me when I say that each and every one of you has given me far more than I could ever give you."

Uncle Hank had to rest a spell. He was getting so tired that he was having trouble setting up in his chair. After a few minutes rest and another drink of water he said, "Well that's about all I have to say except that my life here on this ranch has been the best part of my ninety-three years here on this earth. It's all of you, Thelma, Lewis, Brady and Chance that I should be thanking, for all you have given me. And though I don't say it much I love you all like you was my own flesh and blood." Then Uncle Hank sat back in his chair and took a long breath and relaxed. He had said all he had needed to say.

Lewis looked over at Thelma; tears were running down her face. She, like him, realized that Uncle Hank was saying good bye. Thelma got up and walked over to Uncle Hank and knelt down in front of him and put both arms around his neck and cried like a baby. Uncle Hank hugged her back as hard as his tired old arms could and he cried along with her.

The boys were both watching their mom and they looked over at their dad as if to say what was wrong. Their dad just looked down at the ground as the tears hit his feet.

Then the boys looked at each other as what was happening hit them both like a ton of bricks. Brady slowly got to his feet and went over and knelt down by his mom and hugged her and Uncle Hank and cried. Chance was stuck to his chair too weak to move and just cried.

Rachel and Jeni both went over to comfort their future husbands. They had both started to cry as soon as they saw the first tear running down Thelma s' cheeks. Even the twins were crying though they were too young to truly understand what was going on. Tears flowed like water.

Even though Uncle Hank had always put on an act of a crusty old man who didn't care about anybody or anything but his bottle of whiskey, everyone knew that under that old worn out hide of his, beat a heart that was as gentle as a mom to a new born child. He had never spoken a word in anger that anyone could remember. It was amazing that a heart as big as his could even fit in that tiny frail old body of his. He truly was loved by the Walkers and all who knew him.

It was half an hour before the tears slowed down and everyone could compose themselves. Uncle Hank finally held up his hand so he could get every ones attention so he could say something.

Everyone quieted down and dried their eyes as best as they could and listened to what Uncle Hank had to say. Uncle Hank asked them if he could have some time alone with his buddy hatch. He had said all he had to say to the Walkers and now he had some things to say to his dear old friend Hatch while he still had the strength.

One by one they all came over to Uncle Hank and gave what they all knew would be their last hug. Each one, saying his or her, own personal goodbye, before heading to the house. Thelma was the last to come by. Once again she bent down and put both arms around his neck and gave him a big hug. Uncle Hank reached up and gently wiped the tears from her face. Then he took her face in both of his tired old hands and looked into her eyes. All he said was, "I love you Thelma," and then kissed her on both cheeks.

Thelma did her best to control her crying, but she would cry for days to come. With all the strength that she could muster she got up on shaky legs and brushed off her dress and took a slow deep breath. Then she gave Uncle Hank one last kiss on the forehead and said, "I love you too." Then she said, "I'm going to make you some fresh buttermilk biscuits you old goat," and turned and walked toward the house. Uncle Hank had tears in his eyes and a smile on his face.

Hanks old friend got up and put some more wood on the fire, then sat down in a chair next to him. Hatch looked over at his tired old friend but didn't say anything. He knew that his dear old friend would say what he had to say when he got ready.

They just sat there and looked at the fire for a while before Hank said anything. When he finally did speak it was in a tired and weak voice. He said, "Hatch ole buddy, I've had a good long life. I've had the love of my life, twice, and I've been part of a family that has excepted me for who I am and loved me as one of their own. I have had some good friends, such as you, along the way as well."

"I've been rich, I've been poor, I've been drunk more times than I can count, I've even kept company with a few women of, and lets' just say, questionable character, a few times." He laughed a little at this as did his friend. "Hell, I've even had to kill a few men who were trying to kill me."

He paused a little and looked at the fire. He looked back at his long life and some of the roads that life had taken him down. And with a smile he remembered back to the day that he rode up on a skinny young rancher trying to pull a calf out of a mud hole. He stopped and gave him a hand. After they got the calf out of the mud the young rancher wiped his hand on his pants then stuck it out to him and said, "Thanks friend, my name is Lewis Walker, what might your name be?"

Hank instantly took a liking to this young man and took his hand and said, "My friends call me Hank." That was the beginning of a friendship that would last for over fifty years. Hank sat there looking at the fire with a smile on his face then he came back from his memories.

He said, "Hatch, I don't think that a man can do the right thing all the time. I can only hope that most people that knew me can forgive me for the wrong that I might have done and love me for the good that I've done. I can only hope that my friends can remember me with a smile on their face when I'm gone."

Hatch said, "Well I'll tell you one thing for sure old friend, there will be plenty tears at your funeral. I've never known anyone, who got to know you, that didn't like you. That, my friend, says a lot about what kind of a man you are. I've never known you to tell a lie or be mean to a single soul in the whole time that I have known you. But, I will tell you one thing for sure, and that is, that you are about as cantankerous as that old mule of yours." With this they both laughed out loud and Hank had trouble catching his breath.

After he was breathing a little easier, Hank took as deep a breath as he could, and said, "Old friend, would you please go get me a blanket, my old bones are tired and cold?" Hatch said, "Why sure old friend." Then he got up and squeezed his hand for what he knew would be the last time and gave him a big smile and walked off to the house.

The Wilsons' had gone home. Lewis and the boys were setting on the porch but no one was talking. Hatch slowly walked up the steps and stopped beside Lewis and gave him a gentle squeeze on the shoulder then went on in the house. Thelma was in the kitchen pulling a pan of butter milk biscuits out of the stove when he walked in. She set the pan on the top of the stove then wiped her hands with the rag she had used to take the pan out with. Then she straightened out her apron and looked at The Reverend. All he said was, "Hank would like a blanket."

Thelma said, "Why of course Reverend," and went into her bedroom to get one. She came out with her favorite one that her mother had made for her when she was just a little girl. As she walked over to give him the blanket she said, "If you will wait just a minute while I put some butter and jam on a couple biscuits for him. I would appreciate it if you would give him those as well." But as Thelma reached out to give him the blanket, he put his hand on her shoulder and tenderly smiled at her and said, "Why don't you take the blanket and biscuits to him yourself." Her chest felt like someone was standing on it.

She did her best to not lose control of her emotions. She took a deep breath but couldn't speak for the lump in her throat and simply shook her head slowly. She put the blanket down on the table, and with trembling hands, she put butter and jam on a couple biscuits then wrapped them in a towel and picked the blanket up again. She held the blanket close to her chest took a deep breath then walked out on the porch.

She stopped beside Lewis and he stood up. She handed him the towel with the biscuits and took his hand. They looked in each other's eyes but no words were spoken. Then they walked down the steps and out to where Uncle Hank was setting by the fire. As they walked up to his chair his eyes were closed and his breathing was slow and so shallow that they could hardly see his chest rising and falling. Thelma gently reached down and laid the blanket on his lap and pulled it up to his chin. He slowly opened his eyes and looked up at Thelma and Lewis.

Thelma put her hand on his forehead and smoothed back his thin grey hair and said, "I brought you some biscuits Uncle Hank." He smiled weakly at her, then, the smile slowly faded away as Uncle Hank took his last breath.

14

THE NEXT MORNING THELMA had breakfast ready early just like any other day. The only difference was that instead of the usual ham and eggs and fried potatoes there was only a big pan of buttermilk biscuit in the middle of the table. There in Uncle Hanks spot at the table was a plate with two hot steaming biscuits on it. Lewis came in and the boys came in shortly afterwards. They all sat down and even though no one was hungry, they each buttered up a biscuit and ate in silence.

Thelma was the first to speak. She said, "I think Uncle would be happy if he had known that we are going to put him to rest up on the hill next to your folk Lewis." Lewis and the boys just nodded their heads in agreement. The boys would spend the early morning digging the grave while Lewis made a pine coffin to put him in. It had been a night without sleep for the whole Walker family. The Reverend had gone into town to spread the news of Hanks passing.

Thelma had dressed Uncle Hank in his best shirt that she had made for him and his best coveralls. She even put one of the string ties on him that she had bought for the boys first date. She smiled when she thought how he would have fussed about that. She brushed his hair then kissed him on the forehead and then said good bye for the last time. Lewis and the boys gently laid him in the coffin and put the lid on and nailed it down.

It was around noon when Lewis and the boys finished hooking up the little cart behind Uncle Hanks' mule Gypsy. They thought that it only fitting that Uncle Hank took his last journey with his beloved mule and friend leading the way. When they brought his coffin out Gypsy turned her head around to smell it. She knew that her friend was in it. She let out a loud whiny and pawed the ground then she turned around and hung her head. You could tell that she was mourning her friend.

Lewis slowly led Gypsy up the hill to the small cemetery. Thelma walked behind the cart with her two boys at her side. As they got close to the grave site Lewis could see a cloud of dust in the direction of town. By the time they got to the gravesite the cloud of dust was bigger and by now a line of cars and trucks could be seen that seemed to go all the way back to town.

The Wilsons were in front and then the Henderson's next with Adam driving. Mr. Ramirez was there along with Mr. Dobbs the banker along with just about everybody that the Walkers had ever known. And of course Reverend Hatcher was there. He had spent most of the night spreading the news of Uncle Hanks passing.

Everyone quietly gathered around the grave site once Uncle Hank was lowered into the grave. Thelma stood next to her husband in her new dress. Brady and Chance stood to either side of their parents with Jeni and Rachel at their sides.

Uncle Hank was well known by most folks as a man that enjoyed a good bottle of whiskey. That was the reason for at least two dozen bottles of whiskey lying all around the grave site. There were all kinds of bottles, from homemade moonshine in an old mason fruit jar, to the finest store bought whiskey that money could buy. Even the Reverend had brought his old friend one last bottle.

The Reverend gave a short simple sermon. The fact that there were so many people there, that said what needed to be said. Hank had been the kind of man who liked just about everyone he ever met. He always tried to see the good in people until they forced him to see otherwise. It was always important to him for people to like and respect him. He always figured that if someone didn't like him, then he hadn't tried hard enough to be liked.

The crowd slowly made its way by to give their respects to the Walker family. Then most of the crowd headed to their cars and back to town or home. Even the Wilsons left figuring that this was a day for the Walkers to have their own time to grieve. Mr. Henderson came by and shook hands with the boys and then Lewis. He told Lewis that the materials and lumber that Uncle Hank had ordered and paid for would be there in about a week. Mr. Dobbs came by and ask Lewis if he and the boys could come by the bank when they were up to it. Lewis said that they would come by the bank first thing in the morning to take care of whatever business needed to be done. He knew that Uncle Hank would want things to go forward as soon as possible.

The crowd slowly thinned out and everyone went home except for the Reverend. He just couldn't say good bye as fast as the others. Thelma came over and put her arm through his arm and led him off with the rest of the family as they all headed back down to the house, except for Gypsy, she refused to move an inch from the grave site. She just lay down next to the grave and that was where she was going to stay until she had a mind to move.

Once everyone was settled down on the porch, the reverend stood up and held out a bottle of whiskey. He said, "I would like to propose a toast to my dear old friend, Hank Henry Sterling." He asked Thelma if she would get some glasses. She went into the house and came back out with two glasses and handed them to him. He took at the glasses and said, "I think we need a couple more glasses Thelma." Then he looked over at Brady and Chance and then back at her. She looked over at her boys and then at Lewis. He nodded his head slightly then she looked back at the reverend and said, "Well I guess your right Hatch ole buddy," with a big smile, then she went back in the house and came back out with three more glasses. She gave one to each of her boys and kept one for herself. And then, with a big smile, stuck out her glass and said, "Lets' have that drink shall we boys."

Everyone was dumb struck. No one had ever seen her drink a drop in her life. Hatch looked at Lewis, and he just shrugged his shoulders. Then he poured everyone a drink, but he only poured half as much into Thelma's glass, that he poured into the men's glass. Thelma said, "Don't be bashful Hatch ole buddy," and held her glass up for him to pour more into it.

He looked around at Lewis and the boys then he smiled and filled her glass as full as theirs was. Then he held his glass out and said, "I would like to give a toast that was one of Hanks favorites. Over the teeth and through the gums, watch out stomach here it comes." Then he downed his drink in one big drink. Everyone followed suit, even Thelma.

She coughed and choked and tears came to her eyes as she tried to catch her breath. Everyone was laughing and Lewis was patting her on the back while she was coughing and trying not to laugh too hard. When she finally caught her breath, she smiled and said, "Now that went down as smooth as silk." Then they all broke out laughing till they had tears in their eyes.

After Thelma had quit laughing and had caught her breath she said, "Well if I didn't know better I would say that you boys have done this before." She didn't miss the short little looks that the boys gave their dad, and then the Reverend. Her smile melted away as she held out her glass for Hatch to pour her another round.

He looked over at Lewis who was looking at something on the ground as was the boys about now. He poured her another glass full and she sat down in Uncle Hanks' old rocker. "Ok boys," she said, "Somehow I think that I'm the only one around hear that hasn't heard this story already, and something tells me that its', gunna be a whopper." Then she smiled big and laughed. That broke the ice and everyone broke out laughing along with her.

It was a few minutes before anyone got the nerve to start the story but Brady finally started to speak. He told her the story of the day at Wilson's Creek but he left out a couple embarrassing parts. He still gave her enough details that she could fill in the blanks just fine own her own. Even with Brady's cleaned up version of the story she laughed several times during the story. She could just imagine how embarrassed the boys must have been that day. After all she was a woman and she knew how girls think.

After Brady finished the story she downed the last of her drink and said, "Well, I can see why you boys wouldn't want to tell your mom that story." Then she started laughing again. The boys were beet red by now. Then she said, "Hatch ole buddy, that's some pretty good stuff you got in that bottle, her voice getting just a little slurred, "How about one more round before I call it a night." They all laughed and had one final drink to say good bye to Uncle Hank. It was to be the first, and last time, that Thelma would ever drink whiskey.

Thelma was up bright and early the next morning. She appeared to be just fine but her red eyes gave her away. They were red and puffy from a combination of, too much whiskey, and a long night of tears. She went about her daily routine of fixing breakfast for her family as always.

But today, she had all the trimmings to go along with the biscuits. There was, ham and eggs, fried taters, flapjacks and a big pan of gravy for anyone that wanted to have biscuits and gravy. Uncle Hank had loved biscuits and gravy. She even had his plate set out for him in his spot as usual. This would be a habit that she would never stop doing.

Lewis and the boys sat down and fixed their plates to eat, but they all three, just kind of played with their food not really feeling like eating. Thelma looked up from her plate and looked around at each of them. Then she said, a lot louder than she intended to, "Now you three listen up, I am not gunna have you three sitting around here, like some little boy that has lost his puppy. I want all three of you to eat, a man sized breakfast, and then go out there and do, a man's' days' work. Uncle Hank didn't leave his life's fortune to a bunch of lolly gaggers. Now eat up and get out of my kitchen." Then she got up, threw her apron on the table, ran to her room and slammed the door.

The boys were shocked. They looked at each other and then their dad. Brady started to say something but Lewis held up his hand to stop him, then he said, "Your mom's right boys, we got us a lot of work ahead of us and we had better eat up and get at it." They ate in silence, and when they left the table, there was hardly a scrap of food left.

An hour later, Thelma came out of her room to find her husband and boys gone. She felt bad for the way she had spoken to her family. But in her heart she knew that they understood and weren't mad at her. She went to the door to see if she could see any of them, but there was no one around. She knew that they were going to put in, one of many, a very long day.

She went back to the table and picked up her apron and started putting it on, when she noticed a piece of paper, sticking out from under Uncle Hanks' plate. She slowly picked it up, unfolded it, and read what was inside. "We miss him too Sweetie, Love you, Lewis." PS, Great Breakfast Mom. We love you too, Brady and Chance. She smiled and folded the note and put it in her apron pocket, where she would keep it till it was worn out too much to read. She went about her house work with a big smile. Oh how she loved her family.

As she was doing the breakfast dishes she kept looking out the kitchen window, hoping to get a look at one or all of her boys. Then she noticed that the truck was gone and remembered that they had to go to town to take care of

Uncle Hanks' affairs and sign paperwork at the bank for Mr. Dobbs.

Lewis and the boys were about half way to town when they came across Rachel and Jeni headed in the direction of their ranch. They stopped in the middle of the road to talk to them. After Lewis explained that they had some important business in town that couldn't wait, he encouraged the girls to go on and go to the ranch and visit Thelma. He thought it would do her good to have company. The girls gladly agreed and drove on towards the Walker ranch to visit with Thelma.

Lewis and the boys went on into town, and the first place they stopped was the Bank. Mr. Dobbs greeted them with a big smile and a warm hand shake. He was expecting them and had all the paperwork ready to sign. Mr. Dobbs went through all the details of what Uncle Hank had gotten him to do in behalf of the Walkers. They were all still amazed at how Uncle Hank had kept his wealth, and plans, such a secret all this time. He had never once given them any idea about what he was up to.

Lewis and the boys finished up signing all the papers that needed to be signed, and thanked Mr. Dobbs for all his help. Next they headed to the hardware store to see Mr. Henderson. They needed to find out the details to what all Uncle Hank had done and arranged for them at the store.

Adam saw them come in the door and went to greet them. He was a new person and was fast becoming one of the most popular men in town. It was also the beginning of a friendship, with the Walkers, that would last a lifetime. The Henderson's, would be forever grateful to Brady, for giving them back their son.

As the Lewis and his boys were shaking hands with Mr. Henderson, Adam had excused himself and walked out on to the front sidewalk of the store and was talking to two young children. There was a young boy of about ten and a girl that looked to be about twelve or so. Lewis noticed that as Adam was talking to the kids he reached into his pocket and pulled out, what looked like, a twenty dollar bill, and tried to give it to the little girl, but she wouldn't take it at first. Adam said something to her and pointed to the little boy. Then he offered her the money again. This time she took it. You could tell by to look on her face that it was a hard thing for her to do. Then Adam said something to her and she shook her head yes, then her and the little boy left.

When Adam walked back in the store, he noticed that they were all watching him, and he got a little embarrassed. This being nice to people was a whole new experience for him but he was enjoying every minute of it. He told the Lewis and his boys that those two kids were a couple orphans that had jumped off a rail car looking for food and shelter.

It was a hard time in America, and small children suffered right along with the grownups. Countless families lost everything they had during the Great Depression. It was estimated that upwards of two-hundred and fifty-thousand homeless kids roamed the rails and streets of America at any given day during the hardest times of the Depression.

Adam said that he didn't know their names but he finally convinced the girl to take the money so they could get something to eat. He said that he thought that the little boy was her brother because he had never seen her let go of his hand. He said that he thought she was afraid that they would get separated if she did.

Adam said that he had tried to get them to come to their house but they were afraid of strangers. He said there was no telling what kind of hardships they had been through already and he didn't want to push too hard and frighten them off. He said it took three days to get her to take the money. He figured hunger had finally pushed her as far as she could go. She said she would take the money, only because the little boy would cry his self to sleep at night because he was hungry.

They got down to business as Mr. Henderson showed them the list of building materials that Uncle Hank had already bought and paid for. He told Lewis that there was already enough material, bought and paid for, to build a house, a barn, and then some. Plus, Uncle Hank had set up a prepaid open account for any extra or unexpected things that might come up.

Lewis and the boys were studying the list of material when Lewis, all of a sudden, said, "Extra, unexpected" then he walked over to the store window and looked out at the two small children, sitting on the store sidewalk, eating apples. Then he looked back at his boys, and Adam, and his dad, and with a big smile, he said, "No I don't think there will be any, extra material, at all by the time we're done." Then he smiled real big at them all. The boys looked at each other then back at their dad. They knew what he had on his mind. Brady looked at Mr. Henderson and smiled and said, "You know I think dads right, we're gunna need all the material we can get by the time were done out at the ranch."

Mr. Henderson started to say something but then it suddenly hit him as to what they were talking about. Then Adam smiled a big smile as it became clear to him what they were talking about. Then he walked over to Lewis and said, "Mr. Walker, you and your boys are about the finest people I have ever had the honor to know. Then he hugged all three of them.

They got all their business taken care of with Mr. Henderson. He said they should be seeing lumber in about a week or so. Then the boys started loading up their truck with things like nails, tools, door hinges, hand saws and all kinds of hardware they would need for building the new house. Adam said they could even load up his truck and he would bring it out later after the store closed for the day. Lewis told the boys that he had a few errands to run and for them to load up all they could and to meet him at the church when they were done. They boys had no idea what their dad was up to, but by the look on his face when he left the store, it was going to be big.

Lewis made several stops. He went by the Courthouse, the Sheriff's office, the Post Office and a Lawyer's office. Then he went to the Church to talk to Reverend Hatcher. After he talked to the Reverend for a few minutes he told the Reverend not to tell the boys what they talked about and to tell them to wait here until he gets back. He told the Reverend that he would be back as soon as he could. He said that he had something important to do. Reverend Hatcher just smiled at Lewis as he was leaving. He had a pretty good idea what he was up to and hoped he could pull it off.

15

It was early afternoon when Thelma saw the truck coming down the road towards the ranch. She knew her husband and boys would be hungry so she started to walk back in the house to get supper started. The truck was pulling into the yard as she started to go back in the house. But as the truck passed the house in a cloud of dust and pulled up to the barn, she noticed that the boys were setting in the back on the top of the load of supplies, instead of in the cab with their dad. She thought that this was a little strange and turned around to see what was going on.

She slowly walked down the steps and started walking to the truck to see why the boys were riding outside on top of the load. As she got closer to the truck, Lewis slowly opened the door. He sat there for a little bit before he got out. If she didn't know better, she would have sworn he was talking to himself, because the boys were getting down from the back of the truck and he was up front by himself. As Lewis stepped out of the truck, the big grin and funny look on his face made Thelma stop dead in her tracks. When the boys walked up next to their dad, they had that same silly look.

She had a feeling that those silly looks were about to tell her something really big.

Thelma was nervously wringing her hands in her apron as she walked up to Lewis and the boys. She stopped in front of them and said, "Lewis, boys, would one of you please tell me what those silly looks on your faces is all about." They were all standing in front of the open door, behind Lewis. She couldn't see inside the truck. Then Lewis and the boys slowly moved to the side so Thelma could see what was behind them.

She looked at all of them as she stepped up a little closer. Her mind was expecting everything from a new puppy to a cat or some other abandoned animal. She was not prepared for what she saw when she stepped closer and looked inside the truck. Her heart rose to her throat and she couldn't breathe when she saw two of the dirtiest saddest looking little faces, looking back at her. She had her hand over her mouth when she looked at Lewis. She was speechless.

Lewis came over and put his arm around her. She was shaking and her eyes were filling up with tears. Then all she could say was, "Oh Lewis" He smiled real big, and said, "Mrs. Walker, I would like for you to meet, Rosie, and Jessie Crawford. They are going to be our house guest for a while if it's all right with you."

Then Lewis turned to the kids, He said, "Kids, I would like for you to meet Thelma." Rosie, after a quiet and lengthy pause, finally said, "Hello Mam." Jessie just nodded his head a little at her. Thelma looked at the kids, then at Lewis, and straightened herself up and gently slapped Lewis on the arm and said, "Lewis Walker, what do you mean, if it's ok?" She gently reached in the truck and took Rosie by the hand

and said, "You kids come on to the house with me." Rosie hesitated for a second, and then she looked Thelma in the eye and said, "Ok, we will come with you but we might not stay very long. I have to think on it some before I decide if we like it here." Then she coaxed her little brother out of the truck. She took him by the hand and led him along with her and Thelma.

As Thelma started walking to the house with the children, she turned around to the boys and said, "Would one of you boys please bring their things to the house for me." The boys looked at their dad, then he quietly said, "Their wearing what they own Thelma. That's all there is." Thelma shook her head in understanding, and led the kids to the house. "And, by the way Rosie, it's Thelma, not Mam." Then she gently squeezed her hand and smiled at her. Thelma smiled to herself, as she thought about what Uncle Hank had kept saying, his last few days, bigger house, bigger house indeed.

Thelma led Rosie and Jessie on into the house. She had them set down at the kitchen table. Thelma stepped back a couple steps after the kids had sat down. She quietly studied their faces for a couple minutes before she spoke. Then she walked over and sat down in a chair across the table from the children. Lewis was quietly standing by the door leaning on the door frame quietly listening and watching.

Thelma said, "Ok kids, as she looked from one to the other, I'm gunna make this real simple. I don't know anything about you two except your names. For now, that's enough for me. No one here is going to ask you a bunch of questions about where your from or what has happened to you that has led up to you not having a family or a place to live. It's up to you to talk about anything, anytime you want to, whenever you are ready. Right now, all that's important is for you both to be safe and have a place to sleep that you are comfortable in, and to have a hot meal whenever you're hungry, and clean clothes on your back." Thelma paused a little, while the kids had a chance to take in what she was saying.

Then after a couple minutes she continued. "Well ok now. The first thing we need to do is to get you two cleaned up and fed, if you're hungry? Do you kids like buttermilk biscuits? I've got a hot pan of biscuits in the oven and I'm gunna fry up some chicken too. You kids do like fried chicken I'm guessing? I was just getting ready to put some on the stove when Lewis came driving up in the yard a few minutes ago with the wonderful news of the two of you."

Thelma looked over at Lewis and said, "Lewis, would you and the boys get some water heating up so Rosie and Jessie can get cleaned up?" Lewis smiled at Thelma and said," we're way ahead of you Ma, Brady and Chance are getting two tubs of hot water ready as we speak for baths.

Thelma smiled at her husband. She wasn't at all surprised at him already getting things ready. They seemed to share the same brain sometimes by the way they seemed to be thinking about the same things at the same time. Then she looked back at the kids and said, "Well Rosie, Jessie, do you two want to take a nice hot bath and get all cleaned up?" Rosie looked at her little brother then leaned over and whispered something in his ear. This went back and forth for a few minutes. After all the whispering was done, Rosie said, "Yes Mam, we both agree, she looked at her little brother as if to say there was no use to argue about it, that we, both, need a bath. It's just been so long since either one of us had a bath that we can't remember when it was. And we don't have anything to wear except what we have on. Someone stole what extra clothes we did have a few weeks ago."

Lewis, still standing at the door, cleared his throat to get Thelma's attention. Thelma looked over at her husband, who was smiling like he had just found a pot of gold at the end of the rainbow or something, and said, "Yes, what is it Lewis?" Then Lewis stepped back out the door to the porch and then came back in and walked over to the table and set two, brown paper wrapped packages, down on the table in front of Thelma. Thelma looked at Lewis with a look that said, what is this? Lewis didn't say a word; he just smiled as he walked back over to stand against the door frame with his hands in his pockets.

Thelma looked at her husband and then at the packages again and noticed the names on them. Then it hit her as to what was in the packages. She got up and went over and took his face in her hands and said, "Lewis Walker, you are something else." Then she gave him a kiss on the cheek and went back and sat down at the table.

She looked at the kids and said, "Well Rosie, I think you might find something in this that might come in handy." Then she slid the package with Rosie's name on it across the table to Rosie. Then she slid the other one over to Jessie. Rosie looked at the brown paper package, and then over at Lewis, and back at Thelma. All she could say was, "For me?" Thelma said, "Yes that's for you, now how about we get to those baths." About that time Brady stuck his head in the door and said, "Mom, the tubs are ready." Thelma smiled at her son then stood up and walked around to the other side of the table and gently took Rosie by the hand and said, "Are you kids ready for that bath now?"

Rosie slowly got up while clutching the package tightly to her little chest with one hand and took Thelma's hand with her other one. Then she said, "Yes mam I reckon we are." Then Jessie picked up his package and took Thelma's other hand and followed them outside to where Brady and Chance had two tubs full of hot water waiting behind some tarps that they had strung up to give them both a private bathing area. They even had some canvas on the ground in front of the tubs to give them a clean place to stand while getting in and out of the tub. They even had an old crate by each tub to serve as a table.

Thelma led each child to one of the bathing areas and held back the curtain while they went inside. Then she closed the curtains and left them to their baths. Lewis had brought Uncle Hanks old rocking chair out for Thelma to sit in while the kids took their baths. Thelma set back and waited for the sounds of them getting in the water. After a couple minutes and no sounds of splashing water from the kids getting in the tub, Thelma got up and walked up close to the curtain that Rosie was behind and softly said, "Rosie, sweetie, are you ok? Do you need some help?"

Thelma leaned in a little closer to listen and she could hear Rosie quietly sniffling and crying. She slowly opened the curtain and stepped in and bent down next to Rosie and put her hands on her shoulders and slowly turned her around to face her.

She gently raised Rosie's chin with one finger so she could look her in the eye. Thelma said, "What's the matter

Rosie?" Rosie dropped her package and rushed into Thelma's arms and started crying uncontrollably. Thelma hugged her back but didn't say a word and let her have a good cry. Thelma cried right along with her.

After Rosie had just about cried herself dry she slowly let go of Thelma and stepped back and bent over and picked up her package. All she said was, "Thank you, Mrs. Walker." Then she turned around and set her package down on the crate by the tub. She looked back at Thelma and smiled a small smile then turned around and slowly started getting undressed. Thelma dried her own eyes then stood up and straightened out her dress and left Rosie to her bath.

Then Thelma stepped over to Jessie's bath area to listen for sounds of water splashing. Not a sound was coming from the other side of the curtain. Thelma leaned in close to the curtain and said, "Are you all right in there Jessie?" No answer came back. She repeated herself, still no answer. Slowly she pulled the curtain back to look inside. She had to put her hand over her mouth to keep from laughing. There stood Jessie, in the middle of the tub, with all his clothes still on still holding his package to his chest.

She composed herself and reached out her hand to him. He just looked at her with that big frown of his hand but wouldn't take her hand. So she stepped back and left him alone in the tub. She couldn't even imagine what these poor children have had to endure in their short little lives. She would have to let them do things at their own pace. Time, they just needed time. Like the old saying she thought, "Time heals all wounds."

After a few minutes Thelma heard Rosie say something. She went over to the curtain and said, "Yes Rosie, do you need something sweetie?" After a short silence Rosie said, "Yes Mam, I need a little help with my hair." Thelma opened the curtain and stepped in. What she saw made her want to cry and laugh at the same time. What she saw was a totally different girl than the one that arrived at the ranch less than an hour ago. What she saw now was a beautiful little dark haired girl in a beautiful blue dress just like the one that Lewis had gotten her. But sticking out of all that beautiful brown hair was a new comb that must have been in the package that Lewis had gotten her. The poor thing probably hadn't combed her hair in months and it was so full of tangles that she couldn't get the comb out.

Thelma asked her if she would like some help with her hair. Rosie didn't even look up or answer. She just shook her head yes. Thelma slowly and carefully worked the comb loose and started to work the tangles out of her hair. Rosie began to transform into one of the most beautiful young girls that Thelma had ever seen. After about half an hour Thelma stepped outside the curtain and looked at her husband and boys, and with a big smile said, "Gentlemen, I would like to present the new, and beautiful, Miss Rosie Crawford. Then she reached in, pulled aside the curtain, took Rosie by the hand and led her out for everyone to see.

Lewis had brought out a big mirror out of the house so Rosie could get a look at herself all cleaned up and in her new dress. Thelma led her over to the mirror so she could take a look. She just stood there speechless and stared at herself. With tears in her eyes she ran to Lewis and gave him a big hug. Then she gave him a kiss on the cheek and said, "I've never had a new dress before." Then she gave Thelma a big hug. As Thelma was hugging Rosie she suddenly said, "Jessie, we forgot about Jessie."

Thelma went over and took a peek through the curtain. There he stood, just like a statue the way he was when she last checked on him. Rosie came up behind Thelma and poked her head through the curtain and looked at her little brother. She said, "I'll talk to him." As Thelma stepped out Rosie stepped inside and closed the curtain. You could hear whispering but you could tell that Jessie wasn't about to change his mind. Then all of a sudden you could hear a lot of splashing and Jessie sounded like he was drowning by the way he was coughing and gasping for air. After it sounded like he had caught his breath, there was a little more whispering and then Rosie stepped out from behind the curtain.

She had water all over her new dress and she even had water on her hair. She straightened her new dress, stood up straight, and smoothed her hair down and said, "He's changed his mind about that bath now. He'll be done shortly." And then with a big smile she took Thelma by the hand and started walking to the house. Thelma put her other hand over her mouth to hide her giggling. Lewis and the boys had to walk away to hide their laughing.

16

Half an hour later, Rosie was helping Thelma set the table for supper and the boys were helping their dad unload the pickup in the barn. Thelma looked over at the door when she heard something behind her. There stood Jessie, all clean and wearing a brand new pair of Overalls and a new shirt. Rosie looked around and then went over and took her little brother by the hand and led him over to a chair at the table. After he sat down she said, "Now that didn't hurt did it?" He didn't say anything but shook his head yes.

Rosie went back to helping Thelma while Jessie just sat there quietly with that same mad look of his.

Thelma looked over at Jessie then leaned down and quietly asked Rosie, "Is he always mad like that?" Rosie looked over at her little brother for a minute then looked back up Thelma and said, "Yes mam, he's pretty much like that any time we are around people. He's ok when it's just me and him. We've been through a lot these last few months. I can't remember the last time he laughed or even smiled." Then Thelma looked over at Jessie one more time. All she could say was, "I'm so sorry."

Life got really busy on the Walker ranch after Uncle Hank's passing and the arrival of Rosie and Jessie. The Walkers lost one dearly loved family member but it seems that they may have gained two new ones. Brady and Chance were working long hard days with the new tractor and bulldozer clearing land for building sites and for new fields to plant crops in. Some days Rachel and Jeni would come over, when things were slow at their ranch, and help with work around the ranch.

Thelma and Lewis were getting quiet attached to the girls these days. They were hard working simple girls who weren't afraid to jump in and tackle whatever chore was thrown at them. Lewis spent most of his time getting things ready to build the new barn and then the new house for Brady and Rachel to live in after they got married. He had gotten Chance to clear a nice little spot for the house and he even had him level out around where the house was going to be built for a nice yard and a spot for a vegetable garden.

Reverend Hatcher and Adam had come out and helped some too. Adam would bring out a load of building supplies and stay to help out for a few hours whenever he could. The Reverend seemed to get a little comfort from being around his dear old friend's family. Things were just not the same with Uncle Hank gone. He hadn't had a touch of whiskey since he had that final toast with the Walkers after Hanks funeral. It just wasn't the same.

Rosie was Thelma's shadow most of the time and Jessie was never far from his sister's side. Jessie started to change a little after a few days. He was realizing that he was at a place where he was safe and no one would ever hurt him as long as he was with the Walkers. No one pressured him to talk and he could do whatever he wanted without someone yelling at him. It also helped that Lewis reminded him a little of his own dad, just a lot nicer. He wondered if it was wrong for him to think things like that. He was young but he had been through a lot and seen a lot.

One day Jessie ventured out to the corral to where Lewis was standing with one boot on the bottom fence rail and his arms over the top rail. He walked up a few feet away from Lewis to see what he was doing. He noticed Lewis was looking at that old mule of theirs they called Gypsy. Lewis had seen him walk up out of the corner of his eyes but he didn't turn and look at him. Without turning and looking at Jessie, Lewis said, "That crazy mule has hardly eaten anything since Uncle Hand passed away. I've tried everything from carrots, corn, potatoes, and turnips and I've even tried some of Thelma's buttermilk biscuits."

Lewis opened the gate to the corral and walked over to Gypsy and scratched her behind the ears. He spoke softly to the old mule, "We miss him too old girl, we miss him too." Then Lewis turned and slowly walked out of the corral leaving the gate open. Lewis walked pass Jessie but didn't look at him. As he passed he said, "I think she could use a friend." With that same mad look of his, Jessie just looked at Lewis then at that old mule standing there with her head down. He stayed there by the fence while Lewis slowly walked back to the house.

As Lewis walked into the house he walked on into the kitchen where Thelma was teaching Rosie how to make Buttermilk biscuits. Thelma turned and smiled at him and Rosie gave him a big smile and said, "We are making buttermilk biscuits Mr. Walker." "I can see that. It looks like you got more flour on your dress than you did on the biscuits." He laughed and then turned and went back into the living room to his desk, where he had the plans and blueprints for the new barn and house laid out. He sat there lost in his thoughts for half an hour or so when Thelma walked up and put her hand on his shoulder and squeezed it gently. He was so lost in his thoughts that he hadn't heard Thelma walk up to him or call his name.

He reached up and gently squeezed her hand and said, "I'm sorry, did you say something?" She said, "I just thought that you would want to see this." She took his hand and led him to the front door to where Rosie was standing, looking out the front door. Lewis could hardly believe his eyes. There was Jessie, big as day, sitting on Gypsy's back as she slowly walked around the corral. Lewis looked at Thelma and Rosie and said, "How is blazes did he do that? No one has ever ridden Gypsy except Uncle Hank. Our boys never even rode her. And unless I'm blind, the little rascal even has a smile on his face.

Lewis laughed out loud and hugged Thelma and then ruffled Rosie's hair and when he looked down at her he saw a tear running down her cheek. He nodded at Thelma to look down. When Thelma saw the tears she bent down and said, "Oh sweetie what's the matter?" Rosie turned and hugged both of them at the same time and said, "He's smiling, he's smiling. I can't remember the last time he smiled." Then she ran out the door to the corral. She climbed up on the fence and looked at her little brother and then looked back at Thelma and Lewis with an ear to ear grin and waved back at them.

With tears in her eyes, Thelma took her husband's face in both her hands and gave him a big long kiss and said, "I love you Lewis walker. Thank you so much for being who you are." Then she walked back to the kitchen to finish cooking dinner. Lewis walked into the kitchen with his hands in his pocket and walked over and reached for a biscuit, but all he got was a slap on the hand. "Dinner's almost ready Mr. Walker," she said. Then she gave him another kiss on the cheek.

Lewis said, "How in blazes did he get Gypsy to let him get on his back?" Thelma said, "Well he came in the kitchen and whispered something in Rosie's ear, then she asked me, if she could give Jessie a bowl of sugar. I didn't ask what it was for I just said that it would be all right. He took the bowl and ran out of the kitchen like his shoes were on fire. After a few minutes I looked out to the corral to see what he was doing. I watched him lead Gypsy over to the corral fence and set the bowl of sugar down on the ground. As she nibbled at the sugar he scratched her behind the ears and then slowly got up on the fence. Then he scratched her on the back and slowly put one leg then the other one over on her back. She never even looked up when he did. That's when I came and got you." Lewis just shook his head and turned and went back to his desk and his work. Thelma walked over to the door and looked out to the corral. She just shook her head. They were both on Gypsy's back now. She went back to her cooking.

17

Brandy and Rachel hadn't set a date for the wedding yet. They wanted to wait until the new barn and their new house were ready before they got married. They wanted to start off with things as simple as they could. Their waiting to get married didn't slow their moms' excitement down any though. The moms had decided to make the wedding dress rather than buy one. Rachel did have to spend some time standing still while Thelma and her mom took measurements for the dress. They were working on the wedding dress every chance they got and they were so excited that you would have thought that, they were getting married and not the kids.

Brady had asked Adam to be his best man, Chance had suggested it, and he had gladly accepted the honor, with tears in his eyes. Adam had become the kind of person that valued the important and simple things in life, such as family, friends, respect, trust, and treating people the way you want to be treated yourself. Adams' parents were proud of the man that their son had become.

All the lumber and materials to build the new house and barn had been delivered out to the ranch. Lewis and the boys had made plans to start building the barn on Saturday morning. It was Adam who had found out about their plans to start building on Saturday and he had quietly spread the word, about the Walkers plans, to everyone he could get a hold of and asked them to spread the word. It was common in those days to have what was called a "Barn Raising," were neighbors and friends would get together and help a family put up all the walls to a house or barn. The Walkers were liked and respected by all that knew them. And they had made a lot of new friends when they had the big bar-b-cue out at the ranch. The walkers were in for a big surprise.

Saturday morning came around and the Walkers were all up early. Everyone was excited to get started on the barn. Thelma had gotten up extra early to get started on breakfast. She knew that it would be a long hard day and she wanted to let Lewis sleep just a little longer. She tried to quietly get out of bed but she noticed that Lewis was already out of bed. Just like him she thought shaking her head.

When she walked into the kitchen, she noticed that there was already a pot of coffee on the stove and the door out to the porch was open. She walked out the door on to the porch and saw Lewis standing out in the middle of the yard drinking a cup of coffee. She could tell he was deep in thought. She pulled her robe up tight around her neck and walked down the steps and out to her husband. As she walked up to her husband and put both arms around him from behind and hugged him. "Penny for your thoughts", she said. He squeezed her hands with his free hand and said, "A million thoughts for only a penny? That's a pretty good bargain don't you think Mrs. Walker?" Then he squeezed her hand again and took a sip of coffee.

They heard some noise behind them and as they turned around they saw Brady and Chance walking up to them. The boys walked up, one on each side of their parents. Brady said, "I wish Uncle Hank was here to see the start of all this." Brady said, "Yea, I'd like to hear him tell us how we were doing it all wrong." They all laughed because they could remember how Uncle Hank would fuss and complain about things not being done the way he would have done it. But they all knew that he did out of love and never out of meanness. He truly loved to mess with people and have fun at their expense. He would have a frown on his face but a smile in his heart. Uncle Hank was truly missed by his family.

Thelma broke the silence. "If I expect to get a descent days work out of you men then I had better fix you a good big breakfast. Any special request anyone?" The boys looked at their dad and then at each other, then they all three answered, almost as one, "Buttermilk Biscuits" They all laughed as Thelma walked off shaking her head and the men all headed off to get ready for the big day ahead of them. This would be one of the biggest days in the lives of the Walker family.

Thelma went on in the house to get started on breakfast. But first she woke up Rosie and Jessie. Everyone worked on a ranch, and today was a big day with lots of work to do for all. No one ever pushed Jessie to work. They just let him know some things to do around the ranch and let him do whatever he wanted to do at his own pace. At first he didn't do anything but set around or play with Gypsy. He just needed time to get comfortable around people and learn to trust someone other than his sister.

Who, on the other hand, absolutely loved to help out wherever she could. She especially loved to help Thelma cook and got excited when she would show her something new. Making biscuits was her favorite thing to do and she was getting pretty could at it. Although they would come out looking like anything but a biscuit sometimes. Thelma would just smile at her funny little biscuits and tell her what a good job she was doing. The last thing Rosie needed was criticism. She needed love, patience and understanding. And Thelma had all three, plus lots more to offer.

Once while Rosie was helping Thelma in the kitchen she said that she used to help her mom in the kitchen. That was about all Rosie said about her mom for quite some time. Thelma didn't pry or push Rosie for information about her family. She knew she would talk when she got ready. Or maybe she never would. Either way it was her decision.

Brady and Chance pulled the tarps that was covering up the lumber off and started getting all the tools ready for the day ahead. Tools were simple those days. There weren't any power tools to speak of. It was mostly hand tools in those days. Hand saws, hammers, hand drills, block and tackle for lifting, and old fashion muscle and sweat. The work may have been a lot slower, but the craftsmanship and pride in what you did resulted in the building of houses and barns that would remain standing for generations to come. Doing it right was more important than doing it fast in those days all though, whenever they would have one of these, "Barn Raisings", you would see a lot of work done in a short time.

Lewis was going over the blueprints for the barn to check and see if he had missed anything. Even blueprints and plans were usually just hand drawn plans drawn up by whoever did the building. There wasn't a lot of building codes and Government regulations to deal with. Most people built their own houses to fit their own specific needs. Life was much simpler in those days. Brady and Rachel had help in the design of their new house. Lewis had taken their ideas and put it all in a simple, workable plan that was basic but met their needs. The Walkers were simple people who had simple needs.

Lewis was so deep in thought that he barely heard someone walk in behind him. It was Brady. Brady said, "Dad, you got to see this." As Lewis got up and walked over to the door, he looked outside to see what Brady was talking about. It was still early and the sun wasn't even up all the way yet. You could see the headlights from cars and trucks headed towards the ranch. There must have been twenty or thirty cars coming down the road Lewis thought.

Lewis walked out on to the porch then down the steps and out into the yard as the first car pulled up to the house. It was the Wilson family. Behind them were Adam and his folks and then Reverend Hatcher. They just kept on coming. Mr. Ramirez pulled up in one of his big cattle trucks that he had used to pick up the cattle from the ranch with. It was covered with canvas and when he came to a stop he got out and gave a big wave then opened up the back and twenty or so people started climbing out of the back.

Rachel and Jeni came over with their parents to where Lewis and the boys were standing beside their dad. You didn't have to tell them what this was all about. The Walkers had been part of many a "Barn Raising" and were usually the first ones to jump in to help someone in need. Everyone shook hands and the girls both gave Lewis a big hug then they hugged their future husbands. Then the girls walked over to the porch with the boys to where Thelma was sitting, wiping away the tears. Their mom had already set down beside her and was hugging her. Her tears were soon replaced with a big smile as the girls both hugged their future Mother-in Law.

Lewis walked around and tried to greet each one of the people that had showed up to help but there was a lot of people here. Some he had never met, so he introduced himself to those. You didn't take this kind of generosity and kindness for granted. It was a simpler time where friendship meant something and you didn't look at the world with the attitude that you deserved any more than you were willing to work for.

After Lewis had greeted most everyone, he went in the house and got the plans and drawings for the barn and brought them out to a table on the porch and spread them out as his boys and a few others gathered around. As they studied the plans, Mr. Wilson said, "Lewis, I think you're going to need more plans", as he looked around the yard at all the people and then back at Lewis.

Lewis looked at Mr. Wilson then he looked at the all the men and women and kids milling around in the yard and looked back at him. He said, "I do believe your right, there are enough people here to build two or three barns." Brady spoke up, "Dad, I've studied the plans for the house and I think I can handle that if you want to tackle the barn." Mr. Wilson said, "Yea Lewis, I've built a few houses and I would love to work alongside my future son-in law." Then he smiled real big and patted Brady on the back.

Lewis said, "Sounds like a good plan to me," and with a big smile said, "I'll get the plans for the house." Lewis stepped back in the house and grabbed the house plans and brought them out and handed them to Brady. And as he handed them to Brady, he held on them just a little before he let go of them and said, "Besides, if you mess up on the house it won't be my hide that gets nailed to the side of the barn by the future Mrs. Brady Walker, it will be yours." Then everyone hooted and hollered at that and several of the men patted Brady on the back as they all laughed at his expense. Brady laughed too, but not quite as much as everyone else. If he wasn't nervous before, he certainly was now.

Then Lewis and Brady started dividing the workers into two groups. Trying to split up the most experienced men so both groups would have a good crew that wasn't lop sided with too many inexperienced workers. Chance wanted to work alongside his brother and Rachel and Jeni would be right there beside their men working just as hard as they did. Adam was going to work along with his Dad on Lewis's crew. Adam and his dad had come to be about as close as a dad and son could be. And Thelma of course would make sure that no one went hungry this day.

18

Mr. Ramirez had roasted a whole pig and a young steer the day before and had brought them out in his truck this morning. He had gone over and talked to Thelma and she had showed him where to set things up. And once all the women unloaded all the different food that they had brought, Thelma's worries about feeding this crowd disappeared. About all that was left for Thelma to do was to keep the coffee going. And a few women had even brought their own coffee pots along.

Adam had seen little Jessie standing on the porch by himself kind of hiding in the shadows not talking to anyone. He walked over to him and asked him if he wanted to help work on the barn with him. Jessie just frowned, his famous big frown, and shook his head no. Thelma had been watching, and quietly listening as Adam talked to Jessie. She watched as Adam straightened up and started to leave and called him over to where she was standing. When Adam walked over, Thelma whispered something in his ear. Adam smiled real big and shook his head in understanding.

Then Adam walked back over to where Jessie was standing. He just stood there for a couple minutes rocking back and forth on his heels with his hands in his pocket, not saying anything. And then without looking at Jessie, and not speaking to anyone in particular, said, "I sure wish I knew someone who could ride that old stubborn mule Gypsy. We're gunna need someone who that old mule won't kick or bite when we get ready to start raising the walls on the barn. That sure would make it a lot easier if I could find someone to ride her and help pull those walls up. Then Adam started slowly walking off down the porch steps. As he walked away he could, just barely, hear Jessie say, "Gypsy won't bite or kick me." Adam didn't stop or turn around. He just grinned and kept walking. Thelma was grinning too.

A lot of the folks were working harder than they had worked in a long time. But at the same time they were having more fun than they had had in years to. There's nothing like hard work and good company to make you forget, if only for a short time, all the hardships and troubles in your own daily lives. Like the old saying goes, "Out of Sight, Out of Mind" you could say.

And sadly, some of the folks would eat more today than they had all week. Hunger was still a daily battle for thousands of people in those days. After all the Great Depression still had most of America by the throat and would have for years to come. As bad as things were, most of the people here today would look back on this day as one of the best days they had had in a long time. Today, they would enjoy life, tomorrow, well that was another day.

It looked like a Hornet's nest that day on the Walker Ranch. Lumber flying here and there, hammers banging, saws cutting, people talking and laughing and some of the smaller children were running everywhere and getting into everything. And you might hear an occasional curse word when someone would hit the wrong nail with a hammer. A lot of the folks were working harder than they had in a long time but they were having more fun than they had had in a long time. There's nothing like hard work and good company to make you forget, if only for a day, all the hardships and troubles in your own personal lives.

As bad as things were most of the people here today would look back on today as one of the best days they had had in a long time. Some of the young children would get to be children with any worries and no hunger, if only for a day. Tomorrow they would be back to sleeping on the ground in tents or in some ones barn or worse. Not knowing where their next meal would come from. Today they were all happy and as content as they could be. Tomorrow was another day.

Lewis, along with Adam and his Dad, laid out the plans and details as to how it would be best to get started on the barn. One group would start sorting the lumber as to size and another group would start cutting boards to certain lengths while yet another group would start nailing walls together on the ground then stand up complete walls as a group. That's where Jessie and Gypsy would come in handy to help stand the walls up.

Brady did pretty much the same thing with his volunteers as his dad did. Mr. Wilson noticed that Brady would casually look over at his dad's project from time to time, without being too obvious about it, to see how he was doing things. Brady didn't want to, as the old saying goes, "Get the Cart Ahead of the Horse". Mr. Wilson just smiled to himself but didn't say anything.

Brady's crew really didn't need the help of Jessie and Gypsy to stand up the walls to the house because the walls in the house were much shorter than the ones in the barn and easy to do with just a few men by hand. But it would do Jessie some good to be a part of something that would make him feel good. So whenever he would bring Gypsy over to ask if they needed help Brady would put Jessie to work.

Today Rosie had actually gotten more than ten feet from Thelma's side for the first time since she had been on the Walker ranch. At first it was as if Rosie was Thelma's shadow. Thelma even had to be careful not to step on her when working in the kitchen because she would be so close under foot. But it was no bother to Thelma because she was glad that she could give Rosie a feeling of comfort and safety that must have been missing in her life for some time. At first Thelma would even set in a chair by Rosie's bed and hold her hand until she went to sleep because Rosie would have nightmares at first. But today Rosie was a child again enjoying the sounds and laughter of other children.

Both Rosie and Jessie were starting to act like happy normal little children once again. Even though Jessie still wore his famous big frown most of the time you could tell he was a much happier kid than he was on that first day when Lewis brought him and his sister home. Rosie said that he had always been like that but she knew he was happier here with the Walkers than she had ever seen him.

The children weren't the only ones doing better these days. It seemed that the arrival of the children on the ranch had been good for all of the Walkers. It seemed to help ease the pain of losing Uncle Hank. You could never replace the love of someone like Uncle Hank or fill the void that he left in every ones heart but you can, add more love to your heart, to help in the healing. Uncle Hank would always have a place in all their hearts and Thelma would always set a place at the dinner table for him just like he was still there. She would even talk to him and tell him about the progress of things on the ranch. She even told him about Rosie and Jessie. She knew that he would fall in love with the kids just like the rest of the family had. Thelma was happy, she was content with life, and she was rich beyond measure.

It was a tiring and long day for everyone on the Walker ranch that day. By the end of the day just about everyone there had worked harder, laughed louder, ate more and had more fun than they had in a long time. Even some of the younger children who were too young to do much at their own homes seemed to get in the mood of things and did their best to help out. It seems that moods are contagious, and on this day the mood was all about friendship, kindness, sharing and helping someone in need. There wasn't any fighting or bickering or angry words this day. This was a day of enjoying the best things that life has to offer. This was a day of equals, of respect, friendship and love. This was a day to remember. And few would ever forget that day at the Walker ranch.

By the end of the day the barn had all four walls and the rafters put up. The house had most of the walls but no roof yet. After all, the barn was basically just four straight walls and a roof. But the house was a little more complicated with a lot more walls and doorways and windows to be framed in, and there would be a walk around porch once it was all finished. Even with the amount of work left after this day of hard work from all their neighbors and friends, it had saved

Lewis and his boy's weeks of hard work if they would have had to do all the work by themselves.

That's just the way things were done back in the days when life was simpler and people weren't lost in their own selfish worlds and friendship and generosity were the everyday rule and not the exception. It was a time where the poorest person could be as rich as the next person with the things that mattered. It was a time where people, like Lewis and Thelma, could, and would, teach their children what was truly important and of value in life.

As the last of the cars and trucks slowly headed home, Lewis and Thelma along Brady and Chance and Rosie and Jessie sat on the porch and watched as the last of them disappeared into the darkness of night. Thelma leaned up against her husband who sat on the top step of the porch leaning on the post. As she sat there looking around at her tired and worn out family, she smiled to herself because she knew how truly blessed she was to have such a wonderful family. Lewis was watching her look at their family and he could almost read her mind. Judging by the look on her face she was as proud of them as he was.

He gently reached up and brushed her hair out of her face and said, "We are rich in many ways Mrs. Walker, but our greatest wealth is sitting right here on this porch with us". Thelma looked up at her husband and put her soft hand on his tired, dirty face and said, "You're so right Mr. Walker, I just wish Uncle Hank was here with us. After all, none of this would have been possible if not for him and his big heart and generosity".

Brady said, "Mom, Dad, Rachel and I were talking today, and we decided that when, and if, we have a son we are going to name him Hank. It's just not the same around here without a Hank running around". Thelma got up from her place beside her husband and went over and hugged her son and gave him a kiss on the check. And then, with tears in her eyes, said, "That's the kind of things that makes me so proud of my family. Uncle Hank was so proud of all of you to because he knew that what you all truly valued is the important things in life, the things that real dreams are made of, "Dreams of the Heart."

www.ingramcontent.com/pod-product-compliance
Lightning Source LLC
LaVergne TN
LVHW092048060526
838201LV00047B/1298